The School for Gifted Potentials

Orientation

By Allis Wade

To Amy for your encouragement
To Isabel, Sophia, Harold, and Ginny for your honesty
and
To Isaac for insisting on a series

Acknowledgements

I would like to acknowledge Kazimierz Dabrowski and his Theory of Positive Disintegration, along with other theorists that have contributed to gifted education, which provided much of the impetus for this book.

"Orientation is a book that will appeal to the entire gifted community– kids, their parents, teachers of gifted students as well as gifted adults who have struggled with understanding their own giftedness. Many parents, I suspect, will use the book as a way to help their own children learn about social-emotional issues and how to deal with them."-**Lisa Conrad, Gifted Parenting Support**

"The plot is fast moving and gets increasingly intriguing as the story builds, but there is a goal beyond simply entertaining. The more important purpose of Orientation is to educate young, gifted kids about their unique emotional needs. Since Everett is experiencing an orientation at a gifted school, readers will feel like they are attending class alongside him, learning about overexcitabilities, gifted characteristics, and communication skills."-**Ian Byrd, Byrdseed**

"In her book, Orientation: The School for Gifted Potentials, Allis Wade has skillfully brought together the factual research of a past psychologist with a prospective world of the future, to create a unique book available in today's gifted world: a novel. It is simply refreshing to take a break from textbooks and journals to find oneself riding an emotional roller coaster along with the characters in the book."-**Melinda Gindy, Board Director: Australian Association for the Education of the Gifted and Talented**

"The purpose of this book is to give gifted children a chance to see and better understand themselves in modern literature. They may relate to some of the overexcitabilities described, and even utilize some of the coping mechanisms. Also, gifted children may identify with the attempt to hide their abilities out of a desire to fit in. They may become more willing to accept who they are and what they're capable of becoming."-**Sarah Wilson, Homeschool Review**

<u>Table of Contents</u>

Discovery

The Observer scanned the play pad, looking for unusual and distinctive behaviors. Most of the children were engaged in developmentally appropriate activities and were experimenting with social behaviors such as dominance, compromise, and conformity.

One child stood out to her.

He was playing at the fringe of a group that was building a tower in a sandbox. The children were arguing about the imaginative premise of the shape that they were constructing. The debate centered on whether it should be a control tower or an executive skyscraper. The Observer noted that all three children were conforming to developmentally appropriate roles. She shifted her focus away from them and dismissed them as AVERAGE.

Her eyes flicked back to the boy. She had previously noted that he was arranging small pebbles from the sandbox into lines of ten. Each time that she checked his progress, she could see that he had added more lines.

Grouping objects into tens was an advanced concept for his age and probable level of environmental enrichment and experience. That alone had caused her to mark him as a POTENTIAL. However, as she looked at his lines again, she saw that an even more intricate system had developed. The spaces between the lines of ten appeared to be about two centimeters apart. It was apparent that there was a four centimeter gap after the first ten lines. The initial ten lines were bordered on all sides by a separate set of ten lines. She realized that he was differentiating the lines into boxes of ten lines, and each line contained ten pebbles. To understand the concept of hundreds was yet another piece of evidence that he was a POTENTIAL.

She punched her coordinates into her CNIpad so that a Government satellite could take a picture of what the child was constructing, then uploaded the picture into a file that would be examined at the DETERMINING meeting later that month.

Casually, she stood up and glanced around the play pad. She hoped that she had not given away her interest in the child, although she suspected that he was particularly perceptive and was aware that she had watched him.

She walked around the play pad and tried to appear nonchalant as she scanned each child's identification badge into her CNIpad.

1

The children were accustomed to having their badges scanned by Government officials. Her credentials were appropriately displayed on her chest, her back, and on both forearms of her cream-colored blazer. Several children pointed at her with nervous excitement when they saw the G tattooed at the base of her throat.

The boy arranging the pebbles glanced up at her as she approached. She noted that his hazel eyes rested momentarily on the G, flicked away, and then looked back. He looked her in the eye and then quickly ran his hands through what he had constructed, pushing and shoving the sand into a pile as a child his age would be expected to do.

She pretended not to notice his change in behavior as she scanned his ID badge and walked away.

Everett shifted uncomfortably as he felt the roving eye of the Observer land on him again. He was aware that her eyes lingered on him longer than on any other child on the play pad. She looked at him again and typed something into her CNIpad. Only Government employees had access to CNIpads, which accessed the *Connected Network Interface*, the Government network used to track and store information about its citizens.

Had she noticed the formations that he was creating, or would she mistake them as random play?

His mother would be upset with him if he had drawn an Observer's attention.

She had told him time and again to behave like the other children during his required SOCIAL EXPERIENCE time. He was supposed to select a different group each day and mimic their play. He tried to join in with the other children every day, but inevitably found himself drawn into solitary activities, like comparing the angles in the leaves of a maple tree and creating sets of tens, hundreds, and thousands with small rocks. He could not explain why he was more intrigued by these activities than in the games of tag and hide and seek that had his peers in a frenzy of excitement.

It was just the way he was.

And it worried his mother.

Everett thought of his mother's warnings as he felt the Observer watching him. He was about to switch activities when he saw her get up and walk away. He had just reached one thousand when her shadow covered his creation. He glanced up at her involuntarily and saw the G that marked her throat, looked away from it and then looked back, only for a moment. His hands pushed into the sand in front of him to obliterate what he had created in case it would catch her attention up close.

The Observer's dark eyes narrowed momentarily before her face returned to its carefully practiced impassive facade. He heard the bleep of his badge being scanned and her steps as she walked away.

He spent the rest of his playtime pushing sand into piles, disturbed by the Observer's presence.

Everett was quiet that night at dinner. His mother quickly picked up on his change in behavior and asked him to tell her about his day. They never lied to each other. She was the most important thing in his life, and he was the most important thing in hers. She helped him understand how to process the world and the other people in it.

The people around him all seemed so different, everyone except for his mother. She was the only person that he understood.

He told her that he had chosen to sit near a group of children building a tower in the sandbox, and she nodded approvingly. They were working on a rotation. She wanted him to join in on a new activity at least three days a week, because she said that other children had short attention spans and did not engage in one activity for extended periods of time.

She stiffened when he mentioned that an Observer had scanned his identification badge.

"What were you doing at that time?" she asked guardedly.

He could hear the worry in her voice. Everett wanted to reassure his mother that he had not been doing anything unusual, but they did not lie to each other.

"I was making rows of tens out of pebbles and creating boxes of one hundred because I was trying to get to one thousand. I don't think she noticed because I pushed the rocks and sand into a pile when she came over to scan my badge. I don't think she noticed," he repeated, knowing that his mother was upset.

She did not say anything for a moment, and he knew that she was trying to compose her thoughts.

"Is there anything else?" she asked in a small, scared voice.

"She was a G," he said quietly.

"Oh!" she responded. Her hand flew involuntarily to the base of her neck and then resettled on the table. "I hope that you will try to play with the other children in the sandbox tomorrow. Building a tower could be fun," she finished weakly.

She knew that he did not care for the activities that the other children engaged in. On his first day of EDUCATIONAL EXPERIENCES, he had come home asking her why kids liked to bounce balls and why they argued about turns and rules. When he had tried engaging other kids with questions about the things that *he* wondered about, he had been rejected and ignored.

Everett was an exceptionally attractive boy and was not picked on, but the other children knew that he did not fit in just as well as he did. They allowed him to participate on the fringe of activities, as long as he did not interrupt or try to change the activity. It was an arrangement that worked for everyone, and the teachers were none the wiser. They marked the various activities that he participated in on his checklist, noted the variety of children that he played with, and observed that he was consistently compliant and respectful in all activities.

"I love you," he told her, and he *meant* it. He would do anything for her. He would try again to play in the sandbox the right way.

She smiled at him and squeezed his hand.

"Thank you," she replied softly.

Then she told him about her day and the variety of dishes that she had prepared. She described each in exquisite detail, and they were happy and smiling again by the end of her story.

The event on the play pad was a dark shadow that they both pushed to the back of their minds.

The Observer, Sindra, arrived home that night excited about her discovery of a new POTENTIAL. The number of POTENTIALS in the general population had recently started to dwindle. Most of the gifted had already been channeled into a specialized school or into advanced fields of work.

She was nervous about the data that she gathered. Mathematics was not her strength area, but she had been trained well and recognized that the child's representation of thousands was advanced. Ordinarily, she would have asked the boy to talk about his creation, but the boy had been so guarded.

She grabbed her CNIpad. His behavior was a piece of evidence that she had neglected to document. The five-year-old had been reserved, controlled, and even wary, all characteristics that pointed to an advanced level of emotional development.

Something tickled her brain as she tried to recollect her brief encounter with him. She remembered that he had glanced up at her and then pushed his hands into the sand.

She put the CNIpad down and got up to stretch. Needing fresh air, she passed her hand across the sensor to the door leading to the balcony. It silently slid over to allow her access and then smoothly returned. She placed both hands on the balcony rails and looked out into the night sky. Something about the handsome child was troubling her. As she stared at the glittering stars, she realized what had bothered her about the boy. It was the way that he had looked at her tattoo. She remembered seeing a trace of fear in his wide, hazel eyes when he looked at it.

Fear.

That was an unusual reaction. Everyone viewed the G with a mixture of awe and respect.

Why did he destroy his pattern when he saw the G?

She frowned.

Shouldn't he have been proud to show his pattern to her?

Everett woke up the following morning, elated because it was a BONDING day. His mother did not have to go to work, and he did not have to go to his EDUCATIONAL EXPERIENCES. These were his favorite days. Together they relaxed, talked, explored, and pondered. She taught him things on BONDING days, *real* things that excited him.

He resented that they could not be together all day. They had been, until his second birthday. Mothers were allowed to keep their children full-time for NURTURING from birth to age two. Children had to attend SOCIALIZATION classes part-time starting on their second birthday. Mothers spent that time in job training classes so that they would have job skills by the time their children began their EDUCATIONAL EXPERIENCES, while mothers that had previous work

5

experience took classes to renew job skills that they had once had. Everett had started attending full-time EDUCATIONAL EXPERIENCES on his third birthday, and his mother had gone to work as a chef in a skyscraper restaurant.

Pretending to participate in his EDUCATIONAL EXPERIENCES was painfully boring. He resented that he could not be with his mother more, but she assured him that there was no way around the system. It was the law.

Sighing at these thoughts, he crawled out of his bed and into hers. He nestled into the warmth of her body and enjoyed the rise and fall of her breathing. Something worried his mother, something deep inside of her. He did not know what it was, but he wanted so badly to protect her from it.

Unable to stop himself, he sneezed and hoped that he had not woken her up. Her arm snaked around him, and she gave him a gentle squeeze to let him know that she was awake.

"Sorry Mommy," he whispered.

He felt bad that he had interrupted her sleep, until her gentle squeeze turned into a tickle. He giggled and thrashed and struggled to get free until she turned over and smothered him with a bear hug. As his giggles subsided, she pecked a kiss on his nose and suggested that they eat breakfast. He mimicked her carefree attitude as he padded after her into the kitchen.

Their small apartment only consisted of three rooms. It had a kitchen with an eating counter, a bedroom/living area, and a bathroom. His mother's job was considered SOCIALLY IMPORTANT, so their living quarters were small but adequate.

Although his mother was an excellent chef, she preferred to cook simple meals at home. She often let Everett help cook their meals, and they always ate from the same plate. For some reason, that was important to her.

She said that it made her feel more connected to him.

Everett often saw the shadow of worry pass behind her eyes while they ate together. It made him feel as though their time was measured. He did not understand his mother's worry. Children were allowed to stay with their mothers until they entered the WORKFORCE. They had at least ten more years together, but he figured that she did not see that as enough time.

He agreed.

"What do you say we go on an adventure today?" she asked with a bright smile.

"Really?" Everett squeaked.

They rarely got to go and explore nature. His mother had to apply for an excursion pass and was only allowed to apply every two months. They went as often as they could.

Both Everett and his mother thrived outside. His mother had an endless amount of knowledge about the natural world, and Everett soaked up every morsel of information. As they hiked, she told him about scientific names, taxonomic classifications, adaptations, and symbiotic relationships. They discussed the delicate balance of nature, the importance of predators and prey, birth and death, and feasts and famines.

It made so much more sense to him than the world that he found himself trapped in. He felt that he only fit in the space that he shared with his mother and that nature was a beautiful extension of the bond that they shared. Nature had beauty, mystery, wonder, and the freedom to question and explore.

After a long day of climbing in the mountains, as they returned to their city apartment in a POD, Everett linked his fingers through his mother's and whispered, "Thank you for understanding me."

She squeezed his fingers tightly in reply, unable to speak around the lump that had formed in her throat.

Tricked

Everett's mother saw the anxiety on his face the minute that he arrived home. Her color faded as her heart jumped into her throat. His anxiety changed to anger when he saw her scared, dejected face.

"What happened?" she asked as her hand involuntarily fluttered to her throat.

"I made a mistake today," he ground out angrily.

He was furious with himself, because his carelessness had put that look on his mother's pretty face.

She could not ask. Her mouth would not make the words.

She waited helplessly for him to continue.

His hands clenched into fists at his sides. He did not want to tell her. He just wanted to forget what had happened.

If he did not tell his mother, things would not change.

He was not ready for things to change.

The last four years had been difficult. After the Observer had noticed him making hundreds on the play pad, he had worked even harder to appear academically AVERAGE and socially appropriate at all times. Each day, he purposely made mistakes in all content areas, asked clarifying questions, and even got in trouble every once in a while.

Trying to appear AVERAGE was exhausting.

Today had been different.

Today he had been tricked.

Today he had been challenged.

A new teacher had joined his class and had explained that their normal teacher was at a training seminar and would return the following week. Everett had mimicked the other children's nervous excitement about the unexpected change. They had never had a replacement teacher before.

Everett had been mindlessly stacking cubes into a repeating pattern of 2s and 3s in a learning center when the new teacher had positioned herself on the floor next to him and the two other children at the center.

She had invited the other children to "challenge themselves" to copy Everett's pattern in a positive and encouraging voice.

"Why don't *we* play together?" she asked him conspiratorially as soon as the other children had started the activity.

She began a pattern of her own and carefully stacked 1,3,5,7, and 11 cubes. Excited that he could see the pattern, he added the next set of cubes, 13. A slight hiss of excitement escaped her mouth, and she sat up on her knees as she eagerly set up the next set, 17. He was already a step ahead and was ready with the next set, 19.

He knew that the pattern that she had started was a set of numbers that could only be divided by itself and one. He did not know what to call it, but the rule was entirely clear to him. His excitement faltered when she added the next set of cubes to the pattern.

A sick feeling radiated through him as he suddenly realized that he should not have shown that he understood.

He was about to lay down a set of 22 to throw her off when she said, "Wonderful! Your teacher must not have needed to attend a training seminar after all. She appears to have taught you *all* very well!"

She looked approvingly at him and the other two students as she spoke and did not seem to think that he had done anything exceptional. He felt relieved that he had escaped a close encounter as he walked away.

He was heading to the painting center when he felt a light tap on his shoulder. She was standing behind him with a syrupy smile on her face.

"I'm not sure what your teacher's normal routine is, but when I am in charge of a class, I ask that students clean up after themselves before they leave a center," she admonished.

Everett flushed and slowly pivoted to return to the blocks that he had left out. As he stooped to collect them, he noticed that they were arranged in a new pattern. His eyes quickly scanned the pattern. He was trying to count in groups of ten when it struck him that she had used another method of counting entirely! She had grouped them into sets of three.

He was so excited that he turned to look at her in amazement. Her mouth twisted into a smirk as she leaned forward to speak quietly into his ear.

"Maybe your teacher doesn't need to be in a training seminar. Or maybe you require a different kind of teacher altogether," she whispered.

The chattering and clanging sounds of the classroom faded away as all that Everett could hear was the pounding of his heart in his ears.

Her words repeated in his mind again and again.

How could he have been tricked so easily?

His mother would have shown him this counting system eventually. He should have been nonchalant; he should have scooped the blocks into the bucket and walked back to the art center as if painting was the activity that he looked forward to the most. Instead, he had given a stranger proof that he understood mathematical patterns at a level far beyond his age peers.

He had shown himself.

Everett slowly recounted the events to his mother. There was no point in trying to make them sound irrelevant. They both knew that this was far worse than what had happened on the play pad when he was five. When he finished, she pulled his face into her hands and gazed at him as if for the last time.

Sindra awoke with a start when she heard her CNIpad turn on. A recorded voice announced that she had a message waiting. She quickly logged in and pulled up the message. When she saw that the message was from Eliza, she licked her lips with excitement.

Eliza was from the Board of Mathematically Gifted Individuals and had been sent to interact with the POTENTIAL that Sindra had discovered several years ago. Sindra had sent others to observe him in disguise over the last four years and had carefully collected their observations of his abilities.

Everett was challenging because he was wary of being observed, wary of standing out, and wary of being recognized for academic achievement. His behavior continued to puzzle Sindra, but she had pursued him as a POTENTIAL nonetheless.

"Greetings Sindra. I went to your POTENTIAL's classroom today and found an opportunity to interact with him in a learning center. He was eager to engage with an intellectually advanced playmate, and I quickly discovered that he understood the concept of prime numbers. That alone would have intrigued me, but on an impulse, I introduced a base three pattern. I saw him working it out, and a profound look of

11

joy came over his face when he figured out what I had done. Although he did not add to the pattern, I am sure that he understood the fundamentals of the system. I know that mathematics is not your strength area, so I appreciate the work that has gone into your identification of Everett as a POTENTIAL. I will contact you in the morning to discuss the next steps, but I thought that you would appreciate getting the information about this candidate as soon as possible."

Sindra exhaled slowly. It was gratifying to find out that she had invested her time in this child wisely.

Her mouth furrowed into a sympathetic frown as she pictured him sitting in a classroom that was still working up to adding and subtracting by thousands. How he must feel with the monotony and simplicity of it!

Sindra could relate. An Observer had discovered her when she was eight. The pride on her parents' faces as they had signed the release form for her to test at The School for Gifted Potentials was still clear in her mind.

She had been nervous, proud, and excited when she had arrived at the school's testing facility. The Evaluators had watched her play, watched her draw, and then had sent her off to eat lunch with some of the students. Most likely, they had observed her there as well.

After lunch, they had given her a pencil and paper test that had been full of interesting questions, puzzles, word analogies, and math patterns. It was more exciting than anything that she done in her EDUCATIONAL EXPERIENCES.

She had felt disappointed when the test ended, but her excitement had returned when they began an oral examination that asked her challenging and open-ended questions. They allowed her to play with word meanings, symbolism, and abstract analogies. Sindra had enjoyed every minute of it.

After the test, she had been sent out to a play pad. Several of the children that she had eaten lunch with were huddled in a small group. They were talking about one boy's idea for an invention and motioned her into the group to help settle a debate that had started. She had never felt so accepted by and interested in other children.

Her mind had been humming with excitement over her experiences when she had joined her parents at the RESULTS meeting.

Her parents' faces had beamed with pride when the Examiner had turned to her and asked, "Would you like to attend The School for Gifted Potentials? You have all of the qualifications, and your parents' approval. All we need is your acceptance."

"Yes. I appreciate the opportunity. Thank you," she had replied.

Her calm words had belied her excitement.

Out of the corner of her eye, she had seen her parents nod in approval of her polite words.

That was the last time that she had seen her parents. They had hugged her tightly, shared a few words of encouragement and advice, and had left.

She had been sad to see them go, but she knew that the separation was a necessary transition. Even if she had continued her EDUCATIONAL EXPERIENCES in a traditional school, she would have had to leave her parents' home eventually.

Moving through the program at The School for Gifted Potentials had been a wonderful and challenging experience for her. It had helped her understand herself in a way that another school never could have. She had connected with her gifted peers and had engaged intellectually with people with diverse interests and STRENGTHS.

She was excited that Everett would soon be able to have similar experiences.

For weeks, Everett and his mother were haunted by what they knew would come. *He* was sure that he could still maneuver his way out of the situation. He figured that they would give him some sort of test, and he would fail it. It would not matter how they tried to trick him. He would *never* show his mathematical STRENGTH again.

Being identified as a POTENTIAL meant being separated from his mother, and *that* he could not bear.

There was an incredible sadness in his mother's touch as she held him now. A perpetual knot seemed to be stuck in her throat, and her easy laugh had disappeared. He could see that she did not blame him for his error. She was not angry or regretful, just so very sad.

It made him ache and ache inside.

He could not understand why the students of The School for Gifted Potentials were removed from their homes. Why couldn't he attend that school *and* stay with his mother? He could not help but remember the thrill of creating true mathematical patterns with the replacement teacher. If only his EDUCATIONAL EXPERIENCES could *always* feel like that.

It did not matter. The brief connection that he had made with the replacement teacher did not compare to his love for his mother. He would sabotage any further attempts that they made to identify him as a POTENTIAL.

It was the only way.

A message from the Office of the Chancellor of The School for Gifted Potentials arrived on the morning of his tenth birthday. The message included a brief complimentary section, followed by an appointment time for a mandatory meeting the following day.

His mother had received and signed for the message. If *he* had received it, he would have hidden it from her and then come up with an escape plan.

Her sadness strangely seemed to disappear when she received the message. She seemed resigned to this next step, and even hopeful. After she put the letter aside, she pulled him into her arms and looked at him with a mixture of awe, pride, and love.

She struggled to start speaking as she worked her way past an enormous knot in her throat and a welling of tears in her eyes.

Exhaling forcefully, she brushed the tears away so that she could look clearly into his eyes as she spoke.

"I love you Everett," she started. "I have loved you your whole life, even before you were born. There has been nothing in my life more important than you, more important than being your mother, and loving you. You are so special."

She broke off momentarily to compose herself again and took another deep breath.

"You are so special. If you could only know how much I cherish you. If you only knew how much I have wanted to protect you and keep you in a nurturing, loving place," she said with a shuddering breath. "Now you will go to a school where you will be accepted, where you will be challenged, and where you will fit in! I just hope that, as you start to make friends that are like you and as your instructors challenge you, you will remember that I kept you from those experiences for my own good reasons. I am afraid that you will resent me for making you go to your SOCIALIZATION time and your EDUCATIONAL EXPERIENCES. I knew that they were boring, but I also knew that at night you would come home to me."

Her eyes pleaded with him for understanding.

He felt confused and buried his face in her neck. He stayed that way for a while before he sat back up to look in her eyes.

"Mother... I love you."

It was all that he could say.

He did not understand what she was saying about the school or why she was worried that he would hate her.

He *loved* her.

"I'm not sure why you're so upset. I am *not* going to pass their test. If I know the *right* answer, then I will put the *wrong* answer. They will think that they made a mistake, and it will be over. I am *not* leaving you!" he declared.

He reached up to push her hair off of her forehead. She burst into tears at his familiar touch and sobbed as she held him tightly. He was scared, but he let her.

They spoke no more of it that day.

On the second day of Everett's tenth year, they traveled in a POD to the center of the capital city. His mother was pale and speechless. He was not worried because he knew that he would fail the test and then they would go home together.

A voice announced that they would arrive at The School for Gifted Potentials in two minutes. His mother's hand clenched his fingers, and despite his resolve that it would be easy to sabotage the test, he clenched back to quell his fear.

They arrived at a building with a large central body that had several stories of window lined bridges connecting it to smaller wings. The School for Gifted Potentials was engraved in the alabaster granite. The words looked so powerful and important that Everett shuddered with fear.

They stepped out of the POD at the landing dock and stood there for a moment together. He started forward, eager to be done with the experience.

His mother pulled him back. Her eyes had locked on the building, and she could not seem to move.

Suddenly, she turned him toward her and crouched down to look into his eyes as if she had made a decision.

"What if you like it here?" she asked.

He was momentarily shocked into silence.

"What? I am going home with you! What are you even-?" he cried.

"Listen to me!" she said firmly. Her eyes were no longer sad. They looked fierce and pained. "Would you like to have friends with large vocabularies, vivid imaginations, and interests like yours? Would you like to have teachers that know more than you do, and if they don't, will have the tools to help you learn more on your own? I thought that I was doing the right thing to keep you. Maybe all that you needed was ten years of love. Maybe now you need a challenge and an experience beyond what I can give you," she said urgently.

"Mom!" he protested. "Mom-please. I know that I can beat this!"

"I know!" she said loudly, then softly repeated, "I know. You can do anything Everett. But let's say that you *do* fail this test and come home with me. Do you want to go back to your EDUCATIONAL EXPERIENCES tomorrow?"

He hesitated for only a moment.

"I want to be with you," he said firmly.

17

She smiled and brushed his hair off of his forehead, their gesture of comfort and love, and said, "You are *so* special Everett."

With that, she turned and walked him into the building.

His mother approached a stiff looking woman at an oblong, pearly white counter and placed his letter on the counter without speaking. The woman gave Everett a canned, congratulatory smile before she turned to enter his information into the system. He resisted the temptation to look around and kept a determinedly surly look on his face as he stared at his shoes. A robotic arm reached over the counter to scan his badge, but he refused to look up at it.

"There you are," the woman said as she handed the letter back to his mother.

She activated a host robot, which rolled itself around the counter and raised high on its tracks to greet them at eye level.

"Good afternoon, Everett and Mae. I am Number Seventeen and will be your host today. I will make sure that you arrive at your testing appointment on time. While Everett is testing, I will give you a tour of the facilities. I can also show you where to find refreshments and other amenities," the robot said.

The robot was addressing his mother for the most part, but Everett interrupted, hoping to appear slow and basic.

"What is your name?" Everett asked the robot, knowing that the robot had already given it.

"I am Number Seventeen," the robot repeated courteously.

"Seventeen is a number, not a name," Everett said rudely, wanting to show the people at the school that he was not someone that they would want to keep around.

His mother applied a small amount of pressure to his shoulder. She knew what he was doing but did not approve of his attitude.

"Thank you," his mother said politely to the robot.

Number Seventeen rolled forward and pointed out information about the architecture of the building, the artists responsible for the art work, and other interesting facts as he led them forward.

Mae pulled Everett down to a slow walk and spoke softly in his ear.

"I won't see you for the rest of the day, so there are a few things that I want you to remember. One, always know that I love you. There has not been a decision that I have made that has not been in your best interest. Two, remember to stay true to who you are. I do not want

18

you to be ashamed of your STRENGTHS any longer. I do not want you to act the way that you did with the robot. I want you to always be who you are, in any situation. Three, I want you to always know that I am here for you, even if I cannot be with you for a little while."

She broke away from him to ask Number Seventeen a question about an art piece. Everett repeated her words in his mind as he puzzled over them. His mother continued to act as though they could not get out of this. They would be going home in a few hours!

The last thing she said caused a knot to form in his stomach.

He told himself that she had only meant the next few hours, but grabbed her warm hand for reassurance anyway.

Number Seventeen led them down several hallways and over a window lined bridge. Everett looked down at the people bustling below him and realized that they were mostly children! Some were rushing, some were lingering, and some were playing around. He briefly wondered what a cluster of boys around his age was discussing but quickly pushed that thought aside and held on to his mother's hand even more tightly.

Finally, they arrived at the testing room door.

His mother wrapped her arms around him tightly and whispered, "You are so special. Remember what I said."

She brushed the hair away from his forehead, smiled tearfully into his eyes, and then allowed Number Seventeen to lead her away.

He watched her go for a moment before he stepped into the testing room.

Results

Everett entered the Chancellor's office ready to see his mother and go home. The testing had been an emotionally draining experience. It had been his best performance of subterfuge yet, and he was so exhausted from pretending that he was only AVERAGE that he just wanted to go home and sleep.

His mother was not in the office. The Evaluators had told him that he would see his mother in the Chancellor's office to go over the RESULTS after he completed the final test.

Where was she?

The Chancellor was a tall, wiry man with a sharply tailored goatee and steely gray hair that was trimmed close to his ears. A vague air of authority hung about him. He sensed Everett's confusion as he searched the room for his mother and kindly motioned him into a chair.

At first, Everett did not want to sit down. He wanted to demand to know where they had taken his mother, but his exhaustion got the best of him, and he finally sat on the edge of the chair.

The Chancellor looked at him silently for a long time, and Everett stared back at him with nothing to say. The Chancellor finally cleared his throat and began.

"Well, Everett, that was quite a performance today. You must be exhausted. We can review your RESULTS another day. At this point, it will suffice to say that you have been accepted into The School for Gifted Potentials. Your room is waiting with a light dinner and all of the supplies that you will need for the night. You have been assigned to-"

"What?!" Everett exploded from his chair. "There is *no* way that I have been accepted. I failed the tests. I don't fit in here. Besides, my mother has to sign her consent for me to stay, and there is *no* way that she did. I am *not* staying here."

Everett looked around in panic.

What was happening? How could he have been accepted?

Where was his mother?

"Everett, sit down please. Please. Thank you. I can see that you have a lot of questions and fear and anxiety. I was hoping that we could talk about this tomorrow, but I can see that you need answers now, and I am willing to provide them. We have been watching you for many years. You have shown many indicators that you were a gifted POTENTIAL in the area of math. We finally gathered enough evidence of your abilities to extend the invitation for you to come here today. You did not make this easy for us. You came here today with an attitude of defiance and opposition. Therefore, I had your testing filmed. I watched as you figured out the correct answer and then purposely put the wrong answer on the second, ninth, and sixteenth question of the first sub test, then the third, thirteenth, and twenty-third question of the second sub test; a different mathematical pattern for each."

Everett clenched his fists in frustration. He could not believe that the Chancellor had so easily discovered the patterns that he had used to skew the results of the tests.

"You realized that we would be suspicious of a test that was completely inaccurate, so you missed just enough to make it look like you are bright, but not gifted. You were very good at this. However, as I watched the video of your testing, I saw that your pencil hovered over the *correct* answer each time before you marked the wrong answer. Using those cues, I calculated an IQ score that describes you as a highly gifted learner in all categories. We have not seen scores like yours from a member of the general population in a long time. You are most welcome here," the Chancellor finished. He sat back in his chair and pressed his fingers together as he waited for Everett to speak.

There were so many things that he wanted to say.

They had tricked him, again!

He wanted to deny the Chancellor's words or demand a retest so that he could miss even more questions.

He wanted... his mother.

"Where is she?" he finally asked, hoping that they would bring his mother in so that he could leave.

"Your mother? Oh, she signed the release form this morning while you were testing and left. All that leaves is *your* acceptance," the Chancellor responded confidently.

Everett's heart thudded.

His mother had signed the release and then *left* him.

Her last words echoed in his mind.

I won't see you for the rest of the day, so there are a few things that I want you to remember. One, always know that I love you. There has not been a decision that I have made that has not been in your best interest. Two, remember to stay true to who you are. I do not want you to be ashamed of your STRENGTHS any longer. I do not want you to act the way that you did with the robot. I want you to always be who you are, in any situation. Three, I want you to always know that I am here for you, even if I cannot be with you for a little while.

He did not understand. They had worked so hard his whole life to avoid his acceptance to this school.

How could she have signed the release?

You are so special. Remember what I said.

Her final words echoed in his mind as he slumped in his chair.

Why would his mother want him to stay?

The Chancellor cleared his throat, pulling Everett away from his pensive thoughts.

"I want to go home to my mother," Everett said, trying and failing to sound authoritative.

The Chancellor adjusted a few things on his desk and cleaned his glasses before he sat forward to speak.

"Everett, someone with your capabilities should have no interest in regular EDUCATIONAL EXPERIENCES. We offer a wide variety of stimulating classes. Based on your test scores, you can take advanced mathematics, study a variety of languages, and learn in a multitude of science laboratories. We offer electives like robotics, engineering, and other interesting classes that are sure to suit your interests and your STRENGTHS. You will benefit from classes that are challenging and interesting to you. You will make new friends, and who knows, maybe a few enemies, but they will all stimulate and challenge you!"

"Then I will go home to my mother, and I will ride in a POD to get here for classes every day," Everett said, thinking that this was a reasonable compromise.

The Chancellor sat back in his chair again.

"I am afraid that your suggestion is not possible. Students that attend this school live here," the Chancellor said firmly. "There is no contact with family. Of course, if you complete your specialized education and earn the rank of G, you may at that point decide to look up your mother and rebuild a relationship. However, many of our graduates do not make that choice. We help our students find their specific STRENGTHS, interests, and talents. By the time that they enter their specialization, they have found the perfect match between their abilities and interests. Many become so engrossed in their careers that they do not find the time to seek out old family members. Of course, those with the EMOTIONAL OVEREXCITABILITY often feel the need to reconnect with old friends and family, and many choose to rebuild those relationships. My point is that it will be an *option* for you, but the feelings that you are having right now will more than likely change as you mature."

Everett could not believe it. The idea that he could ever be so engrossed in an experiment that he would not care to track down his mother seemed ludicrous to him.

He stood up and shook the Chancellor's hand.

"Thank you for the opportunity, but I will return home to my mother. I will manage to become a productive member of society even with the limited EDUCATIONAL EXPERIENCES that I'll have access to," Everett replied firmly.

Everett turned on his heel to leave, but paused when he heard the Chancellor uncomfortably clear his throat again.

"Everett, I didn't want to have to tell you this," the Chancellor said. "I was hoping that you would choose to stay. Your mother has specifically requested that you attend this school. Her request overrides the need for your acceptance. Because of this, you do not have a choice in the matter."

Abandoned

Everett trailed mechanically behind Number Seventeen with his head hung low. Even though Number Seventeen was just a robot, he seemed to understand Everett's demeanor and stayed quiet.

They passed through several hallways before the robot stopped. Everett knew that he would never find his way out of the maze of hallways without the robot's help, but he bitterly realized that he had nowhere to go to anyway.

Number Seventeen told Everett to hold his badge up to a black monitor. It flashed as it verified his number, and the wall in front of Everett slid open to reveal a small but cozy dormitory. He walked in to find a desk, a table, a bed, and a chair. The robot told him to wave his hand in front of a sensor to enter the washing area. A towel, some bottles of soap, and other toiletries were laid out for him, as well as a pair of sleeping clothes that had GP monogrammed on the lapels.

The robot proudly told him that all of his clothing would have that monogram to signify that he was an honored member of The School for Gifted Potentials.

Irritably, Everett wondered *who* it would signify that to. The other students were *all* members of the school, and they only saw each other.

Sighing, he thanked the robot and asked for some privacy. He bitterly cranked the water to the hottest setting as he stepped into the shower and hoped that the steaming water would wash away the sick feeling that had come over him ever since he had met with the Chancellor.

Anxiety coursed through him as he tried to understand why his mother had *left* him. He had never doubted his mother or her intentions before, but now that he did, he felt as though the ground below him had suddenly crumbled, trapping him in the rubble.

Everett still felt anxious and confused as he stepped out of the shower to dry. The mirror had not turned cloudy, despite the steamy shower, and he saw that his skin had been scalded to a bright pink. A grim smile marred his handsome face as he thought that, while the shower had not washed away his terrible feeling, it might have removed a few layers of skin.

He put on the luxurious sleeping clothes and looked at himself in the mirror. He almost felt a sense of pride and hope as he looked at his fine, ivory nightshirt with the royal blue GP monogrammed onto the lapel, until he saw the wet mop of hair lying on his forehead. Not having his mother there to sweep it away from his forehead caused a new knot to rise in his throat, and he angrily swept it away on his own.

He clenched his fists in frustration as he walked crossly back into his room. When he saw that Number Seventeen was still there, he stopped in confusion and stared at the robot.

"I am assigned to your service for the next week to help you acclimate to your new environment. I ordered your dinner while you were away and it has been delivered. I will teach you how to make your own meal selections in the morning," the robot informed him politely.

Everett was annoyed that he did not have his room to himself to sort through his feelings, but once he smelled his dinner and his stomach rumbled in anticipation, he realized that he was grateful for the robot's help.

"So, will you be sleeping here?" Everett asked as he lifted the cover off of his dinner plate.

He noted that the plate was perfectly portioned into the recommended percentages of proteins, fruits, vegetables, fats, and carbohydrates. A sigh caught in his throat as he tried not to think about the food that he should be eating with his mother at that moment.

"When you no longer need me I can go into a "sleep-like" state in which my battery will recharge, however, I can instantly switch back to my operational mode if you need me," the robot replied.

Everett was slightly uncomfortable with the robot's presence, but his conflicted feelings about his mother's choice and his present situation made him crave company, even if it was from a robot that basically responded from a script. He decided to get some answers from his companion about his new home so that he would feel more prepared to walk out of his room in the morning.

"So what will my routine be like? Do I have classes, then lunch, then classes, then dinner, and then more classes?" Everett asked sarcastically. He realized that he was being rude to the robot, but he did not care at the moment that he was breaking his promise to his mother to be polite.

Number Seventeen was instantly prepared with an accurate answer.

"All new students attend a one week ORIENTATION. During your ORIENTATION, you will learn about the CHARACTERISTICS of gifted learners and any OVEREXCITABILITIES that you have. Lunch and snack times will be with the other students, but you will eat dinner in your room during your ORIENTATION so that you have time to decompress and so that you can work on evening assignments," the robot explained.

Everett popped the last of his carrots into his mouth and replaced the cover on his empty plate before he padded back into his cleaning area.

ORIENTATION doesn't sound too bad, he thought as he brushed his teeth.

When he came back out, his plate had already been removed and his bed had been prepared. He smiled inwardly. Number Seventeen was proving to be pretty good to have around after all.

He thanked the robot and told him that he could begin charging. The robot rolled to a corner of the room, plugged into an outlet in the wall, and seemed to fall asleep.

Everett climbed slowly into the unfamiliar bed and realized that sleeping was going to be the hardest part. Going to sleep without knowing that his mother was a hands breadth away; waking up without climbing into her bed for a quick hug.

Hot, angry tears poured from his eyes, but he did not wipe them away. He found their wet warmth comforting in a way as he drifted into a fitful sleep.

Adjustment

The next morning, Everett woke up to find a uniform laid out for him at the bottom of the bed. Number Seventeen was waiting expectantly for Everett to open his eyes.

He greeted the robot absently as he stumbled around in his unfamiliar room to get ready for the day. Number Seventeen explained how to put on the uniform, which was made from fine material and had the same GP monogram as his nightshirt. The students rushing under the sky bridge had worn the same white monogrammed shirt and royal blue vest combination that he now wore.

When he looked into the mirror, he saw a different person, one whose life had changed irrevocably, a Gifted Potential.

As promised, the robot taught him how to activate a touch screen, review a menu of options, and select a healthy breakfast. It arrived quickly at the hands of a different robot. Everett ate hurriedly and tried not to feel nervous about the next few hours.

A thought came to him as he saw the robot waiting patiently for him to finish his breakfast. He'd had limited experience with robots. There were many like the one that had delivered his breakfast that morning that served the public with menial jobs, but he had never really interacted with an intelligent robot that communicated with humans as its primary role. To this point, he had been rather sassy to the robot, who had only been helpful to him.

"I was wondering if I could give you a nickname. We will be spending a lot of time together this week, and Number Seventeen is kind of formal. Could I call you Sev?" Everett asked.

The robot processed his request for quite a while, because it was not a question that he had been programmed to respond to.

Finally, the robot replied, "You can call me Sev."

It almost seemed to Everett that the robot had made his own independent decision. The robot's agreement felt strange to him, but also good, like they had just bonded.

Everett felt quivery with anticipation, dread, and excitement as he followed Sev back through the multitude of hallways that they had passed through the night before. They paused at the edge of the now bustling main lobby. Students dressed like him rushed by in singles, pairs, and small groups and seemed to be under a deadline. He wondered why, until he heard a distant gong-like sound. The lobby cleared, and Sev explained that it was the signal that the first class of the morning had begun. Everett nodded and followed the robot down a hallway as he wondered if he was late.

Sev pressed the intercom button on the door of Room 187 and announced that Everett had arrived. The robot explained that they had reached the office of Everett's advisor and that he would remain in the hallway during the scheduled visit.

Everett wanted to protest because Sev had become a lifeline for him in the brief time that they had been together.

The door slid open to reveal a young, pretty woman with dark hair and a golden complexion. Her brown eyes were smiling, and she had an excited, almost giddy expression on her face as she invited him in. Her office was spare and orderly. She had no personal pictures or trinkets, just a desk, a few chairs, a communication screen, and a CNIpad.

Everett awkwardly sat down, and with nothing to look at on the walls, he settled on scanning the woman's features. He had been slumped in his chair, but on closer examination of her face, he bolted upright.

He looked at her accusingly and burst out, "You're the G that saw me making patterns of ten on the play pad when I was five! You're the reason that I'm here, *aren't* you?"

Sindra's smile faltered. She had anticipated meeting this POTENTIAL for many years. She was so proud of discovering him and following through on IDENTIFYING him. When Eliza had notified her that he had been accepted to the school, she had requested to take some time away from her duties as an Observer to be able to play the role of his advisor during his ORIENTATION.

She had expected to find him full of relief and gratitude that he had been saved from the tedious EDUCATIONAL EXPERIENCES that he had been subjected to, not full of anger over his discovery. Suddenly, she remembered his reaction to her presence on the play pad and her concern that he had destroyed his creation so that she would not see it. She started talking, hoping to find out why Everett had such an adverse reaction to the school.

"My name is Sindra. I am your advisor and yes, I am responsible for your presence here today. I discovered you on the play pad five years ago, creating rows of tens and hundreds, which I knew was

advanced for your age. You shied away from me when I approa̶
you to see your creation, so throughout the years I have sen̶
Observers disguised as teaching assistants to interact with you. You
put on quite a show. You were masterful at showing *just* enough
engagement and proficiency in classroom activities to appear
AVERAGE, but you never showed your full POTENTIAL in any area.
Your social interactions were the same. You gave just enough not to
ostracized, but never enough to be fully included. It seems like a
rather boring way to have spent the last five years," she said with her
eyebrows raised.

"I *liked* my life. I would go back to it right now if I had that
option, but thanks to you, I am here for good," he retorted. Tears of
frustration welled in his eyes against his will, and he looked away
from her to hide them.

Sindra did not understand what he meant. His words and his
reaction upset her, so she lashed back.

"I am sorry if you prefer to spend your time playacting rather
than learning," she snapped. "I think that you should give this school
a chance before you choose to go back to EDUCATIONAL
EXPERIENCES that are not motivating, not challenging, and not
stimulating. Your POTENTIAL is much higher than I think you realize.
It is about time that you begin to develop your abilities."

After she spoke, she noticed his tears and read his body language.

She regretted her words, but could not take them back.

Everett chose not to explain to her that he was not lazy. He
wanted to be challenged and to learn more from his EDUCATIONAL
EXPERIENCES. He *wanted* to make friends that felt the same way that
he did about words, math, and science.

Living at this school was the problem. In his heart, he yearned to
be at home with his mother, talking about their days, exploring the
night sky with homemade telescopes, and making up funny stories.

How could he share those feelings with the very woman that was
responsible for taking it all away from him? His memories were too
dear to share with a stranger, especially one who had judged him as
lazy and ungrateful without really knowing him.

"Everett, I believe that I have started this meeting with a negative
tone, and I apologize," Sindra said after a long pause. "My role is to
help you begin to feel acclimated here and to help you understand
yourself as a learner. In my opinion, you have been given an amazing

31

opportunity to attend this school, and I can see that our opinions differ. I hope that by the time you finish your ORIENTATION, we will both find that your opinion has changed. Now, I have a brief questionnaire for you to fill out."

For a moment, Everett thought about resisting. How long would they keep him around if he refused to speak or interact?

But then what would happen?

He did not feel that he could go home and face his mother yet. They had never lied to each other, or at least, he knew that *he* had never lied to *her*, and he didn't quite know yet what he would say to her.

Reluctantly, he pulled the questionnaire into his lap and leaned back in his chair to peruse it. Her "brief" questionnaire was over two hundred questions. It asked him to respond to statements like *"I often think about ways to improve items that I use on a daily basis"* with *never, sometimes, often,* and *always.* He sighed and began to circle his responses.

About halfway down the page, however, he sat up slightly in his chair.

The page seemed to be describing him!

Soon, his body was doubled over the paper. The statements in the questionnaire described him again and again and again, things that he had never revealed to anyone but his mother. His brain was shouting YES! YES! YES! as he poured over the document in excitement.

Sindra kept a guarded look on her face so that his attitude would not change because of her excitement, but inside she felt gratified by what his body language told her. The transition had been hard for him, as it was in varying degrees for everyone, but his body language showed that he was identifying with some of the things on the questionnaire and that those things excited him.

Everett felt disappointed when he reached the last question. He wanted to go over the questions again and again, feeling as though they held his identity. Some of the tension that he felt from constantly having to hide how imaginative and creative he was had melted with each honest answer.

Everett pushed the document across her desk and stood up to shake off some of his nervous excitement.

"So what *is* gifted?" he asked her, trying to sound casual and uncaring.

He kept his back to her as he looked at the wall, not wanting her to see how eager he was to find out the answer.

"Well, your ORIENTATION will help you understand that very concept," she replied. "It is a complex topic that cannot be summed up very easily-"

"Try," he interrupted, feeling bold and needing the answer.

"All right," she replied, smothering a smile. "The Government's definition of a gifted learner has not changed much in the last one hundred years, although the way that it *approaches* gifted education has changed considerably. There are several different definitions of the concept of giftedness, but I can tell you about the traits that we look for here at The School for Gifted Potentials."

He nodded tersely to show that he wanted to hear what she had to say.

"Each gifted individual is unique, despite fitting into the gifted category, but gifted people have some CHARACTERISTICS in common. Our students demonstrate exceptional intelligence, a high need for stimulation and challenge, and a dislike of repetitive and remedial tasks. Many have one or several OVEREXCITABILITIES, one or more areas of STRENGTH, and many have a talent. We IDENTIFY students that show extraordinary POTENTIAL in one or more areas, but despite having that in common, our students vary in aptitude, work ethic, interests, and many other qualities. Does that help?" Sindra asked kindly.

Everett did not respond.

None of those things sound bad, he thought.

So why had his mother been so afraid of his STRENGTHS becoming discovered? He had thought that her fear was that he would end up at this school, but then she had abandoned him, so he wondered if there had been another reason that she had wanted him to conceal them.

"Why don't you have any pictures in this room?" he asked, surprising her with a personal question.

"Oh, well, this is only a temporary office for me. I will only be here for your one week ORIENTATION," she replied, sounding surprised at the abrupt change in topic.

Everett shrugged as a response. He felt like he would have personalized the office at least a little, which made him think of his own room. Could he make changes to his room? How long would he be there? When was he going to leave this school?

She smiled as the questions poured out of him.

"Your current room will remain your space for many years, and you will be given opportunities to personalize it. Most of our students stay here while they complete their MASTERY studies. Once you have been given the chance to strengthen your natural abilities, and when you demonstrate advanced learning abilities in all of your strength areas, you will select an ADVANCED field of study, such as robotics or engineering or world languages... there are so many options! You will receive the G tattoo once you have demonstrated MASTERY in your field of study."

She proudly lifted her chin to reveal her own G tattoo.

"You see, you have been identified as a Gifted Potential, which means that you have shown POTENTIAL in a strength area, and we will no doubt begin to see in the next few weeks that you show some of the innate CHARACTERISTICS of a gifted learner. Many of our students come from a family of G and often attend our school from a very young age. We still find gifted POTENTIALS in the general population though, like you, and it is always exciting for us to find them and give them this opportunity. Not all of the students that attend this school complete their MASTERY studies. Therefore, only a small percentage of the population receives the G tattoo at the base of their throat."

"So are you saying that I am not gifted if I walk out of here today? You are only gifted if you complete this program? I thought you said that giftedness is just part of who you are. How can attending or not attending this school change that?" he asked incredulously.

Sindra shifted as she considered his question.

"Essentially, you can say that you only receive the G *tattoo* if you have MASTERED your specialized field of study. I will let you come to your own conclusions about whether that is the same thing as *being* gifted. Now, you have much to do today, as I do. Number Seventeen will bring you back tomorrow," she said as she dismissed him.

Sev was waiting for him in the hallway with a container of water, which he gratefully drank as he followed the robot down more hallways. He noticed that the walls all contained samples of artwork and writing, as well as photographs of students building things, competing in sports, and socializing.

I should start paying attention to these things to use them as landmarks for when Sev leaves me, he thought.

The robot finally stopped in front of a classroom door. When the panel door slid open, Everett saw a teacher and students of a variety of ages.

He hesitated.

This was more threatening than being alone in an office with Sindra.

The teacher was a middle-aged male and was rounder and hairier than the Chancellor had been. Everett had had limited contact with adult males in his life and was unsure of how to act with them. The teacher's eyes creased in the corners as he smiled, and Everett felt an instant connection to him.

He motioned Everett into the room and called out to Sev to join them. He told the robot to stay powered on to record the class and explained that Everett could review any part of the lesson that night by watching the recording. Everett felt relieved and quickly found a seat.

"We were just beginning our discussion of the CHARACTERISTICS of gifted individuals. Please turn to a partner and review your understanding thus far. Kimin, please tell Everett what you understand about the OVEREXCITABILITIES," the instructor said kindly.

Kimin was a petite, pretty girl that Everett guessed was probably seven or eight years old. Her shiny black hair was pulled back with a royal blue ribbon, and her black eyes glowed with excitement over getting to share her thoughts with him. This was certainly not something that he'd had the opportunity to do in his other EDUCATIONAL EXPERIENCES.

"Hi! So, there was this psychologist named Dabrowski," Kimin began. "He lived in a really messed up time, with like wars and genocide, and he was surrounded by people doing terrible things. But he noticed that there were *some* people that he interacted with that were *above* it, like they had a higher moral compass than others."

Kimin paused briefly to pull her legs under her body to sit up on her knees.

"So Dabrowski kept noticing that some people seemed to experience the world *differently*. They *reacted* to things with more intensity, and had an expanded *awareness*, and he called that way of experiencing things the OVEREXCITABILITIES. We call them the OEs," she said with a wink.

Everett nodded to show that he was listening as the girl leaned forward with her hands on her knees.

"Dabrowski identified five OVEREXCITABILITIES; SENSUAL, PSYCHOMOTOR, IMAGINATIONAL, INTELLECTUAL, and EMOTIONAL. The last three were the ones that he thought were the most powerful in leading someone to a higher level of development. Some people have no OEs, some have a couple, and very few have them all. So far, from what we've covered, I've learned that I have the IMAGINATIONAL OVEREXCITABILITY."

Kimin stopped talking and switched her feet back to the floor.

Everett looked around nervously and saw that the other students in the class were still talking earnestly. Kimin had spoken so rapidly that he was sure that there was time for him to ask a few questions before the others finished.

"Thank you, Kimin," he replied awkwardly. "So Dabrowski noticed that some people have intense reactions to their experiences, and he called their reactions the OVEREXCITABILITIES. Of the five OVEREXCITABILITIES, people can range from having none, to having some, to having them all. Is that about right?"

Kimin's jaw dropped.

"How do you do that?" she demanded.

Everett shifted uncomfortably. Now Kimin would act strangely around him, just as his mother had warned.

"Do what?" he replied as he looked down.

"Do what?" Kimin repeated and playfully swatted his arm. "You just summed up what I said in like thirty sentences into two, and you made perfect sense! That was amazing!"

The respect that Everett heard in her voice made him look up in surprise. He saw that her eyes were shining with respect, something he had never expected to receive from another child.

Mr. Dodd excused Kimin to join a small group nearby and took a seat by Everett. He smiled his kind smile again and waited for Everett to say something.

This was a new approach for Everett, and he hesitated. He did not know if he should introduce himself, ask a question, or thank the instructor. Finally, he found a way to do all three.

Untangling his tongue, he said, "I'm Everett. Thank you for letting me join your class. How will I find out what my OVEREXCITABILITIES are?"

Mr. Dodd chuckled.

"Well said Everett. Welcome to our class. I'd like to tell you a little about the OVEREXCITABILITIES, and we can see if you have any questions as we discuss them. How does that sound?" he asked kindly.

Everett merely nodded and smiled back, his first genuine smile all day.

"As you learn about the OVEREXCITABILITIES, I want you to think about *awareness, intensity,* and *range*. With any OVEREXCITABILITY that you have, you will be more *aware* of stimuli, like sensory input, emotions, or ideas. Your daily experience will be more *intense* than other people's. You will experience an *extreme range* in your response to stimuli. For example, your emotional experiences may range from elation to incredible sorrow. When you have an OE, it feels natural to experience life this way, and it might seem strange to you that other people don't function the way you do. However, people who do not have that OVEREXCITABILITY might find it strange that you react to your experiences with such intensity. They might wonder why you don't just "stop" it," Mr. Dodd explained.

Everett nodded thoughtfully. He had always sensed that he experienced life differently than other kids his age, but he had never known that there was an actual name for what he felt. It made sense that it had been so exhausting to pretend to react to things "like other people" because it was so deeply part of him to experience life with more intensity.

His mother had always told him to act like the other children so that he would not end up being sent to this school, but then she had abandoned him with no explanation. Was there another reason that she had coached him to disguise these traits?

"What is your face trying to tell me Everett?" Mr. Dodd asked patiently.

Everett struggled to find the words to explain what he was feeling.

"Why are the OVEREXCITABILITIES a bad thing?" he asked, not wanting to meet Mr. Dodd's eyes.

37

Mr. Dodd's face puckered in confusion.

"Well, Everett, I am confused by your question. They are not a bad thing, not at all. Have I given you that impression?" Mr. Dodd asked, sounding genuinely concerned.

"No! No you haven't..." Everett faltered.

How could he talk to a stranger, even a kind one, about his mother? To explain all of the times that she had coached him to hide his precocity for learning from others, seemingly at all costs? To do that would conjure up questions about why she had abandoned him, which was something that he was still unable to grapple with.

"I just thought, you know, by the title..." he trailed off, knowing that it was a lame finish. He could tell that Mr. Dodd had questions about his real meaning, but would let it slide for the time being.

"As we talk about OVEREXCITABILITIES, please remember that they are a STRENGTH and can be harnessed to do wonderful and amazing things in your brain," Mr. Dodd responded after a brief pause.

Mr. Dodd patted Everett reassuringly on the shoulder and stood up to ask the class to join him for a discussion. The other students wrapped up their conversations and moved their chairs into a rough circle as he began talking.

"Today we will discuss the SENSUAL OVEREXCITABILITY. Think about the five senses and how the brain experiences and reacts to sensory input. Don't forget to consider the *range* and *intensity* of experiences with OEs. With this OE, you will experience pleasure or displeasure from sensory information with a greater *intensity* than other people do. The sensory information will come to you in the form of things that you hear, see, taste, touch, and smell. Does anyone have any thoughts about this topic?"

Everett glanced around the circle in surprise. Was there not going to be a lecture?

Kimin raised her hand with a giggle.

"I really like to eat food!" she exclaimed.

Mr. Dodd nodded.

"Food is a good place to start. People with this OE can derive intense pleasure from eating. They may delight in trying a wide variety of foods and might enjoy particular foods with great intensity. You might enjoy a range of different textures in food, like squishy, chewy, dense, and silky. Be aware that your intensity might drive you

38

to overeat, so be sure to pay attention to the nutritional content of the foods that you select!" he said as he chuckled heartily and patted his ample stomach.

A pretty girl that looked like she was about Everett's age hesitantly raised her hand. She seemed rather quiet and serious and held herself very carefully. Her wispy blond hair was pulled back in a neat bun, and she somehow seemed to wear the school's uniform more neatly than anyone else. Her face flushed slightly when Mr. Dodd encouraged her to participate without raising her hand.

"I actually have a *difficult* time eating foods with a variety of textures. I also feel sickened by the smell of some foods. Does this mean that I can't have this OE because I *don't* like the sensations?" she asked and shyly ducked her head.

Everett got the sense that it was difficult for her to draw attention to herself.

"Excellent question Greta!" Mr. Dodd responded. "As with all of the OEs, you will have extreme highs, which in this case would be extreme pleasure from eating, but also extreme lows, which would be an intense aversion to certain foods. It is the same with different smells. Sometimes you will be *drawn* to intense smells, but you can also be repulsed by other smells."

A tall boy that appeared to be much older than Everett awkwardly cleared his throat and said, "I have always had an intense reaction to what I hear and see, like to music and to some pieces of art. I once saw a painting that was so beautiful that I found myself weeping. I've had the same experience with music. There are some songs, even some particular notes, which move me quite intensely."

Greta and Everett nodded in understanding.

"That is one of the truly wonderful aspects of having this OE, Jeremiah," Mr. Dodd said. "The extreme highs of enjoying a sensory experience can be quite powerful. In fact, you should make it a priority to give yourself time to have rich sensory experiences. We offer an extensive variety of options at the SFGP, such as concerts, art festivals, and a wide range of menu choices."

Everett had struggled to block out sounds his whole life. He could hear sounds that no one else seemed to notice, and a sound could drive him mad until he found the source of it. He understood that enjoying music could be a positive side of this OE, but the connection between his enjoyment of sounds and the frustration that they often caused surprised him.

"I guess I have always enjoyed touching things," he added hesitantly, "but I also get frustrated by things rubbing on me. My hair falls on my forehead, and I constantly have to push it back."

He noticed Greta bob her head sympathetically out of the corner of his eye.

"The sensory input that you take in can bring you incredible joy, but it can also feel frustrating and overwhelming," Mr. Dodd said with understanding. "Because of the *range* and *intensity* of your experiences with an OE, you are capable of both positive and negative reactions to sensory input. You will be more *aware* of the sensory input, and you will react to it with a greater *intensity*. Mr. Elan will teach you some managing strategies that you can use this afternoon. That is all the time that we have for this session. I'll see you soon."

Although Everett did not join in on the good-natured groan that the rest of class emitted, he felt a similar pang.

A Troubling Encounter

Sev led Everett out of Mr. Dodd's classroom to begin a facility tour. They walked over a sky bridge into the Arts Complex, which Sev explained had been one of the first wings added to the school because so many students had identified STRENGTHS in PSYCHOMOTOR, VISUAL, and PERFORMING ARTS.

He peeked into the visual arts studio and saw pottery wheels, easels, and a large space in the back reserved for students working on sculptures. Everett was not sure if this interested him. He had always felt pressured in his previous classrooms to create happy, child-like drawings that did not interest him.

After mentioning this to Sev, he was motioned into the room to look at an easel. It held a large canvas that was filled by a charcoal drawing of a dark gargoyle-like creature. Its head was turned to look slyly at the observer of the piece with its eye narrowed in mischief. An evil smile curved its thin lips slightly. The bulk of its frame filled most of the canvas, but in the background of the piece, there was a scene of a family enjoying a moonlit picnic. The insinuation that the gargoyle was going to cause mischief for the family sent chills down Everett's back. He found himself searching the piece for more clues about what would happen next and kept going back to the look in the Gargoyle's eye.

This was certainly different from the friendly art that his teachers had taught him to create. He found himself amazed at the power of the artist. How could someone capture so much of a story and create so many questions in the mind of the viewer with one simple piece of charcoal? Was it possible that an instructor could give *him* the tools to tell a story like that?

They crossed into the athletic complex and entered a large, padded room that held bars, rings, and other interesting equipment that Everett was unfamiliar with. The floor had a slight bounce to it, and he walked around on the floor for a while, enjoying the sensation that he was floating, and processed what he had seen so far. He thought about the equipment that he had seen and compared it to what he had used in his EDUCATIONAL EXPERIENCES.

Suddenly angry, he turned to Sev and said, "You know, maybe the people who go through this school aren't any more special than anyone else. Maybe they just have the nicest tools to learn with. I think that *all* kids could earn a G if they had this stuff. Maybe the Government should stop favoring The School for Gifted Potentials and give the resources to kids who really need it!"

"Oh?"

The response to his tirade did not come from Sev. It was a female voice, deep and rich, that came from somewhere in the back of the room. Through the sunlight that streamed into the far side of the room, he saw the silhouette of a girl outlined on a beam. Her legs were extended into a split, and she held her body at the perfect angle to maintain balance and form. As he watched, she pushed herself nimbly out of the split into a fluid handstand and then exited the beam with a perfect double flip. She brushed chalk off of her hands as she moved toward him with one eyebrow raised.

The smirk on her face told Everett that she knew more than he did, much more, and he felt uncomfortable. He had never met another kid that could hold anything over him, and he discovered that he did not like the feeling.

The girl was tall, probably about three or four years older than him, and had a long oval face, coppery red hair, and sharp green eyes. She stopped a few feet from him with her muscular arms folded over her chest to show that she was ready for a confrontation.

"Is this your first day?" she asked, although her tone made it sound like she already knew the answer.

Her tone made him stiffen, as if a judgment was being made. Defiantly, he raised his eyes to hold her gaze and nodded stiffly.

She dropped her arms and walked a few paces away to grab her water, as if his response had told her everything that she needed to know.

"Well, then I suppose that you don't know the history of gifted education," she said with a smirk. "Let me give you a rundown so that you don't walk around making statements like that anymore. You see, there has always been a NATURE vs. NURTURE debate surrounding gifted learners. Either we are genetically equipped with the tools that we need to reach our full POTENTIAL, which is the NATURE side, or we need an enriched environment to develop the innate POTENTIAL that we are born with, which is the NURTURE side. For hundreds of years, our Government claimed that we did not need special programming to develop our POTENTIAL, because that opinion saved them a lot of money. One hundred years ago, there was a revolution.

42

Gifted people finally got tired of not being given adequate opportunities to reach their full POTENTIAL. So they developed this school, and children from all over the country come here to receive an education that is commensurate with their abilities. This school does not ask them to wait to learn, or to learn less, or to learn on their own in the corner of a classroom. Our instructors *care* about our goals and our strengths. They help us understand ourselves so that we know how to push ourselves to the highest level possible. We also have *each other*, our gifted peers, to push us, to engage us, and to challenge us. So if you think that this place somehow "steals" opportunities from other learners, you need to learn a little more about the progress that we have made in the last one hundred years and more about the *needs* of gifted learners."

She spoke passionately, and a fire lit up her eyes from deep within.

Everett felt uncomfortably uninformed and could not find the words to respond. He turned on his heel and strode out of the gymnasium with an apologetic Sev trailing behind him.

Once they were in the hallway alone, Everett told Sev that he no longer wanted to finish the tour and needed some time alone in his room. Sev searched through his programming to find a way to deal with this turn of events. The schedule for the day was carefully laid out, and it was the robot's responsibility to see it through.

Everett refused to go down any more hallways and knew that the robot could not make him go. After several attempts to get Everett to finish the tour, the robot relayed a message to Everett's advisor.

Sindra was irritated by her POTENTIAL's attitude when she received the message and stormed over to the Arts facility. She was ready to tell him that he could leave and go back to his old life, until she saw his dejected form in the hallway ahead of her. Her steps and her temper slowed as she approached him. His head hung forward and his shoulders quivered. She could read the sadness in his body as if it was a flashing message. He felt lost and alone and she remembered that it was *her* job to help him adjust to the school.

"Thank you Number Seventeen. You have followed your protocol admirably. Please meet us in the refreshment facility in thirty minutes. I will ensure that he gets there," she promised.

The robot followed her command. As he rolled away, Everett regretted the position that he had put the robot in and vowed to stop taking his angst out on his only ally at the school.

Sindra motioned for Everett to walk with her. He protested when he realized that she was continuing the tour, but she held up her hand to stop him.

"I am going to give you a different kind of tour than Number Seventeen would have. I don't have all of the facts and information that he is programmed with, but I *do* have memories," she said.

She led him out of the Arts complex without further comment and into a hallway of classrooms. Sindra and Everett stopped in the doorway of a classroom just as the students started a heated debate with their instructor. Some of the students took the side of the instructor, while others took the opposing side. Everett looked at the face of the instructor and saw a wry smirk on his face. His eyes were lit up and engaged as if he had *intended* to cause the disagreement.

Everett moved into the doorway, wanting to know more about the debate, and wondered what it would be like to be a part of it. He shrank back when he saw the girl from the gymnasium look up at him with an I-told-you-so smirk on her face. She was leaning back in her chair as she listened to the debate but did not seem to be on either side. Sindra motioned for him to move along with her, and he gladly followed.

She paused at the door of an empty classroom.

"This was the first classroom that I spoke up in," she told him softly. "I was here for almost a year before it happened. I came to this school when I was eight. Before that, I had received EDUCATIONAL EXPERIENCES designed for AVERAGE learners, but unlike you, I did not hide my STRENGTHS. I had a large vocabulary and loved to use it. My teachers were impressed by my verbal precocity and always praised me for it. I soaked up their feedback. I couldn't get enough. Once I came here though, I figured out that they had praised me because I had given them the responses that they wanted to hear. I had never said anything particularly original or innovative, and if I would have, they would not have praised me for it."

She paused for such a long time that Everett started to wonder if he was supposed to say something.

"When I came here," she continued abruptly, "the teachers asked questions that had no right answer. *Everyone's* ideas were accepted. I

44

didn't know how to answer those questions. I hung back and rarely participated. I thought that maybe the test had been wrong. But one day, in this classroom, a teacher asked us if humans should decide which plants were *allowed* to grow and *where* they could grow. They had asked open-ended questions before, but this question riled up an unexpected response in me. I took the side of the plant, saying that people had no right to decide its shape or size or location. Others in the classroom felt that humans have the right because plants cannot defend themselves. I finally got engaged in a debate. We discussed that question for days. At some point, we moved on to another question, but I was hooked after that. Being allowed to freely debate a topic that I was passionate about freed me from my desires to provide the correct answer to a teacher and get praise for it. I knew then that I did not want to learn any other way."

As she recalled the experience, Sindra's eyes lit up with the same fire as the girl in the gymnasium and the instructor in her classroom, the same fire that Everett felt when he learned with his mother. Angrily, he pushed that thought aside.

Sindra looked at Everett out of the corner of her eye to gauge his reaction. At one moment, his face had seemed hopeful, almost happy, and the next moment his face had clouded over.

She shook her head. It was going to take a lot to get through to him, but she knew that one day he would have a moment like hers and would realize that he had come to the right place to learn.

She led him up and down a few more hallways, but realized that he was not even looking at the classrooms anymore and took him to the refreshment area early to wait for his robot. His apathy exhausted her. She saw with relief that Number Seventeen was also early and happily relinquished Everett to him.

Everett remembered his vow when he saw the robot. After a disinterested good-bye wave in Sindra's direction, Everett stood awkwardly at the robot's side and struggled to find the right words to express his regret.

Finally, he said, "I apologize for delaying your schedule Sev. I will try to be more considerate in the future."

The robot shifted slightly, and although he had few features on his face that moved, Everett got the sense that Sev was pleased.

Everett suddenly felt famished and ordered a complete meal. He pulled it out of the terminal in the wall with his stomach grumbling with anticipation and looked around. There was plenty of space to sit. He was relieved that most of the students were still in their classrooms. He had just finished his salad when a crowd of students moved into the area. The noise in the room increased as students lined up at the refreshment terminals and began filling up the tables. He kept his head down and moved to the edge of the table.

He heard his name called out by a young, excited voice, and his head shot up in surprise. Kimin was waving to him with a wide, friendly smile on her face. Everett flushed and waved back. He didn't know what the appropriate response was.

Kimin made it easy for him when she rushed to his table with a few friends in tow. She introduced them to Everett as they surrounded him at the table and then proceeded to chatter incessantly.

Everett felt relaxed and happy to be surrounded by friendly people. He noticed the gymnasium girl take a seat at a table on the far side of the room and interrupted Kimin's chatter to ask her if she knew who the girl was.

Kimin bobbed her head excitedly and leaned forward in a conspiratorial manner to fill him in on what she knew. Her friends leaned forward as well, although they were not sure what the pair was talking about.

"Her name is Diedre," Kimin whispered excitedly. "Her friends call her Dre, but if you're not her friend and you call her that, she takes offense. She is fifteen and has lived here since she was six months old. She is *only* friends with the kids that also started as infants. They call themselves *originals,* and they call us, the ones who came as children, *transplants.* Their parents believe very strongly that children should be immersed in a full-time learning environment essentially from birth in order to fully NURTURE their innate giftedness. Many of their parents went to The School for Gifted Potentials as young children themselves and believe in the opportunity for growth that this school provides."

Everett was confused.

"But I had to take a ton of tests to get in here and some of them used pencil and paper. How did any of their parents know at such a young age that they were even gifted?" he asked.

"Well, giftedness tends to run in families. Like I said, their parents are all G, so the likelihood of them producing a gifted child is super high," Kimin replied. "So they bring them to this school and they are immersed in learning from day one, with colors and patterns and sensory learning, physical development, musical development, language development, everything. I've seen the classroom for the babies. It has stuff to play with and interact with everywhere. Diedre says that it is the *ultimate* way to NURTURE a young child's POTENTIAL. She thinks that kids that don't have the opportunity to learn and grow with that kind of enrichment have been paid a disservice, and she says that *transplants* never reach their full POTENTIAL."

Kimin shrugged as if she did not care if Diedre was right or not and switched to the topic of hydroponic farming. Everett looked back at Diedre's table of *originals* and memorized each face, thinking that he might need the information later.

He finished eating just as Sev told him that it was time to begin the next phase of his schedule. Everett thanked Kimin and her friends for eating with him and followed Sev down yet another hallway.

Everett was soon standing in the doorway of an empty classroom and protested that Sev must have made an error in the room number. He entered at the robot's insistence and was followed shortly by Kimin, the other students from Mr. Dodd's class, and their robots. Kimin playfully teased Sev that he should have told her where he was taking Everett next so that they could have all walked together.

A tall, wiry instructor walked in and pulled a chair over to where the group was sitting and talking. He was much younger than Mr. Dodd and exuded confidence and wit. His brown eyes flashed with amusement as the group quickly scooted their chairs to form a semi-circle around him.

"Good afternoon," Mr. Elan said cheerfully. "I would like to welcome Everett to our class, although it seems like Kimin has already done a good job of that."

The other students chuckled knowingly as Kimin beamed at the perceived compliment.

"Mr. Dodd told me that you shared some of the wonderful experiences that you have had with the SENSUAL OVEREXCITABILITY, and that some of you also brought up the *challenges* of experiencing sensations with such intensity. The SFGP has tools that you can check out to help you with a variety of needs. Some of you *crave* a variety of sensations, while others *avoid* sensations. Many of you will do both because of your range of reactions," Mr. Elan said.

Everett nodded as he realized that he fit into both categories.

"If you *seek* stimulation," Mr. Elan continued, "we have a variety of objects for you to hold and touch. If you want to *avoid* textures and pressures that are distracting to you, we can review the menu to find food choices that are acceptable and can even change the fabric and size of your clothing and shoes."

Hesitantly, Greta asked, "What if I need to block out distracting noises?"

Everett leaned forward, eager to hear the answer.

"First, try to *limit* auditory distractions whenever possible. Two weeks ago, a student complained about the sound given off by the light in her room, so I had that adjusted. You can also find ways to increase your *tolerance* of noises. Begin by doing a pleasurable activity with a low level of an irritating sound and gradually increase the volume or amount of that noise until you begin not to focus on it. Once that happens, start at a low level again, but this time, do something challenging, like an assignment. As before, you can gradually increase the volume or frequency of the noise. In that way you will *desensitize* yourself to it. If you plan to do this, please talk to me and I can help you set up a plan. We can also provide you with specialized devices to wear in your ears. They can be tuned to different frequencies that allow the wearer to focus on particular sounds, such as human voices, and tune out other sounds, like dripping water. These have to be fit to you, so if you would like a set, I can set up an appointment for you," Mr. Elan offered.

Everett and Greta shyly raised their hands for an appointment and shared a smile as their eyes met.

"Now, go ahead and roam through our selection of sensory tools. Try them all and see if something appeals to you. If you would like to discuss menu and clothing options, please see me," Mr. Elan said as he stood up.

Out of the corner of his eye, Everett saw Greta move to Mr. Elan's side to discuss the menu choices. She gestured to her sleeves and grimaced, and Mr. Elan pulled out a few fabric samples for her to touch.

Everett stood up, eager to try out the interesting equipment. He could tell by the way that some of the other students approached the items that they were unsure if they needed a sensory tool, but he knew that he wanted one. His senses both craved and avoided different sensations.

A large selection of tools of varying sizes, weights, and textures were spread out on a table. He immediately disliked the tools that had large bumps and shapes projecting from them. A smooth, metal cylinder caught his eye and felt just right when he rolled it in his hand. It was heavy enough to provide feedback to his hand, but it was not tiring to hold. He rubbed his thumb along the cool, smooth surface and noticed with satisfaction that the friction heated the metal slightly.

Jeremiah selected a multi-colored cube that had a different texture on each face. Kimin and Sonniy joked around with the objects, but it was obvious that neither of them identified with this OE.

Greta and Mr. Elan walked over to the table when they finished going over the menu and clothing choices. She picked up a few items and shyly selected a thin rod that had the shape and texture of a twig. Mr. Elan showed the students how to check out materials and said that they could turn them in and check out different tools at any time.

Everett pocketed his new tool thoughtfully as Mr. Elan announced that the class was over.

Originals

As Everett followed Kimin out of the classroom, an unexpected feeling of pride washed over him as he realized that he had participated in a discussion on the very first day.

Being at this school might actually be great, he thought just as he suddenly tripped.

He found himself sprawled on the floor, and as he looked up, he saw a tall, athletic boy sauntering away from him, sneering at him over his shoulder. Everett recalled seeing his face at the table of *originals.*

The boy had been sitting next to Diedre.

Kimin and Greta reached down to help him up. Greta's face was unreadable, and Kimin's was full of sympathy.

"Don't worry," Kimin said reassuringly. "They always mess with *transplants* during their ORIENTATION. They can identify us because of our robots. I heard that they leave you alone once you no longer have a robot to guide you around, so it shouldn't last long."

Everett brushed himself off without comment and tried to keep his face impassive, but he was boiling mad inside. He had never been bullied by his peers before. He wondered if the instructors knew about the bullying *and* how Kimin knew so much about it.

Seeing that Everett was looking suspiciously at Kimin as she walked ahead with her arm around her friend Sonniy, Greta fell back a step and spoke softly in his ear.

"Kimin has a great knack for observing others. She appears to be bubbly and carefree, but that disguises her natural curiosity and talent for noticing small things that others might not notice. She is a great friend to have," Greta said gently.

Everett nodded to show that he was grateful for the advice. He wanted to start a conversation with Greta but was not sure how to begin. To have been pulled into a social group so quickly and easily felt wonderful to Everett, but he was unfamiliar with making small talk. He was still searching for something to say to Greta when their robots announced that they were at their next location.

"Recreational period!" Kimin and Sonniy shouted as they ran into a large room that had both indoor and outdoor spaces.

Children of all ages filled the room. He noticed that some were taking advantage of a large structure of play equipment, some were hanging out in small groups, and some were playing games that Everett was unfamiliar with.

"What is this?" he asked Greta, although he was pretty sure that he already knew. Recreational time had always felt like torture to Everett at his previous school.

Her solemn, translucent blue eyes held his gaze for a moment before she looked away.

"This is meant to be an unstructured time. There are opportunities for physical movement, for social interaction, for creative expression, and for nature exploration. There is also an independent learning center and even a few places just to nap if you choose. This is in our schedule twice a day," she told him wearily.

Everett realized that she was also a *transplant* and might be feeling some of the same emotions that he was grappling with.

"I'd like to see where you can explore nature," he said, hoping that she would want to join him, but not sure how to ask. He figured that she could just tell him how to find the area if she did not want to join him.

To his relief, she eagerly gestured for him to follow her to the outdoor portion of the rec center. Everett felt an immense sense of relief as he stepped into the blazing sunlight because he always felt more comfortable outside.

The fragrance of plants hit his nose before his eyes had adjusted enough to see them. A lush jungle-like area spread out before him through nearly invisible panels of netting. Greta silently showed him where to scan his badge. Once they had both scanned their badges, one of the nets quickly rolled up, and they darted into the enclosure just before the panel rolled itself back down.

The netting excited him because it indicated that living creatures were in the exhibit. Greta shared a rare smile with him and then led him down a few paths. She pointed out a few camouflaged animals and insects as they walked and then motioned him to a bench that was nestled in a grove of banana trees. Her face was lit up with excitement and anticipation.

He eagerly sat next to her on the bench and realized that she must know that something was about to happen. He heard a soft snuffling sound and the movement of branches. Greta's mouth curved into a smile as she watched the grove of banana trees ahead of her.

Everett watched in amazement as a black tapir slowly ambled through the grove of trees in front of them. Its three-toed feet squished carefully through the mud as it made its way west. Every once in a while, it lifted its long, rubbery nose into the leaves to search for food, and lowered its head with a snort when the attempt was futile.

Just before it left the children's line of sight, the tapir found a few small bananas that someone had attached to a tree. The tapir pulled the whole bunch down with its nose and pushed them slowly into its mouth. Its large teeth crushed the bananas into a pulp as the animal continued on its way.

Everett and Greta shared a smile and breathed a mutual sigh of joy.

"She comes through here every day at about this time. The Animal Sciences students use this area as part of their ADVANCED STUDIES and provide enrichment for the animals here," Greta told Everett.

"Do you usually come here on your own?" he asked.

"Yes. Kimin and Sonniy both use this time to interact with others. I have an interest in science, so I use this opportunity to explore and observe nature," she replied softly.

Everett smiled, and an awkward silence stretched between them until he asked her what he really wanted to know.

"How long have you been here? Where did you come from?" he asked curiously.

Greta remained silent for so long that Everett was afraid that she was not going to answer him. She stood up and started walking down a new path. Everett was unsure if he should follow her, until she looked back over her shoulder and bobbed her head to show that he could join her. He caught up to her and leaned closer as she started speaking softly.

"My home is hundreds of miles away from here," Greta shared. "This is the only school for the gifted in the country, which is why there are so many of us. If we were at a local school, our classes would be much smaller. Our group is small now because it is only for the newest students and they take us at all times of the year."

She paused to take a deep breath and ran her fingers along the rubbery leaf of a plant.

"My parents are both G. My mother studies wind energy, and my father works to preserve local wildlife populations from the encroachment of neighboring farms. They believed that they could provide for my needs as a gifted learner through enrichment at home. We played games, read books, studied science journals, and worked out math formulas together. I thrived when we learned about things that I was interested in, but in a way, it made my EDUCATIONAL EXPERIENCES feel even more limiting. I tried not to show my parents how much I disliked going to school. When they asked me about what I had learned, I tried to make my day sound interesting, but they could tell that I wasn't actually learning anything new. I heard them talking about it at night. They even went to my school to speak with my teachers a few times. The teachers were all very nice and understanding and tried to use some of the strategies that my parents suggested, like asking me open-ended questions, giving me independent study opportunities, and pre-testing me at the start of a unit so that I didn't have to sit through lessons about what I already knew."

Again, she paused as if struggling to continue.

"In the end, though, it was still not challenging enough. They decided that I should meet other kids that are like me so that I can be challenged and form some meaningful relationships. My parents were both students here and they loved it. The *originals* try to make *transplants* feel inferior because of our lack of challenging EDUCATIONAL EXPERIENCES, but my parents said that most of their friends that are G try to keep their children at home for as long as they can. They want the opportunity to bond with their children and to set a foundation for them before they enter this world of perpetual learning and intellectual growth and talent development. My parents want me to develop a strong work ethic and to develop a willingness to take risks in my learning. I know that they think that this school is the best opportunity for me," she finished sadly.

Everett was amazed at how similar their stories were. Her EDUCATIONAL EXPERIENCES were similar to his, and she also loved her family. Her sadness over losing them was apparent in her eyes, which she tried to shield from him, until she saw the same sadness reflected in his.

"It sounds like this place is close to perfect, except for the lack of communication with our families," he said with a frown. "So why aren't we allowed to stay in touch with them?"

Greta was about to answer him when Sev and Greta's robot Number Twenty interrupted them. The robots informed them that their recreational time was over and that they had to report to their next activity immediately. Greta placed a hand on Everett's arm as he turned to follow. When he looked back at her, she was flushed and looking at her feet.

"Thank you for sharing this time with me," she said awkwardly, and Everett realized that she was as unused to making friends as he was.

A shy smile crossed his lips before he hid his embarrassment by asking Sev for water. Their small group converged with Kimin, Sonniy, and Jeremiah. As the group of students and robots entered the hallway, Sev announced that Everett would not be following the others. Each student had meetings set up with different people who would help them develop a deeper understanding of themselves.

Irritated by this news, Everett watched helplessly as his new friends moved away from him down the hallway. He was pleased to note that Greta turned to look back at him with a regretful smile on her face.

Sighing, he turned the other direction to follow Sev. He could not believe that there was more. He felt like this had been the longest day of his life. Once again, he found himself in a hallway full of offices, offices like Sindra's, and he wondered if they were all as blank and barren as hers had been.

His question was answered when an office door slid open and the smell of water, plants, and fish bombarded his senses. His ears picked up the sounds of running water, motors, and rustling feathers. Plants, aquariums, and bird stands covered every available wall and surface in the office.

He noticed the other human in the room last. A gray-haired woman of short stature was bent over an aquarium with her back to him. She looked over her shoulder at him briefly, and he saw a twinkle in her eyes before she turned back to finish feeding a small group of carnivorous turtles. She placed a few worms in the aquarium and turned the turtles to see them before the worms wriggled into the soft sand.

Once the turtles had lazily swallowed their prey, she turned toward Everett and motioned for him to settle into the only

55

uncluttered space in the room, an office chair that looked as if it had recently been cleared.

Her face was not smiling. She sat in her own seat across the desk, pushed her spectacles up to the bridge of her nose, and picked up a piece of paper to study.

Everett shifted uncomfortably in his chair. He still had no idea who this woman was, why he was in her office, and why she was pointedly ignoring him.

Finally, she put the paper down and leaned forward to rest her elbows on the desk. She held his gaze for a few moments before she began.

"Good afternoon Everett. I am Ms. Rosenthal. I generally instruct the ADVANCED STUDY courses in the field of Natural Sciences. I am here because you chose to spend your recreational time in the Nature Center. I am aware that you were with Greta, who was already identified with an interest in science. My purpose is to assess whether you have the same interest or to see if you merely visited that area to make a friend," she said briskly.

He was astounded.

They were watching him?

Why should it matter where he spent his recreational time?

Would he be in a different office right now if he had picked up a ball and tossed it around?

The idea that he had been spied on irked him, so he sat back and pointedly crossed his arms. The woman sitting across from him raised her eyebrows as if she understood his meaning and set her mouth as though she was accepting a challenge. She busied herself with the papers on her desk and never once looked at him to see if he had surrendered. His brow furrowed in irritation as he realized that she had the gumption to wait him out for an eternity. He would have to talk first, if only to get himself out of her office.

"What do you want to know?" he finally asked.

She pushed the papers that she had been reading aside as if nothing had happened and resumed the conversation. A brief, triumphant smile crossed her lips before she spoke.

"I have some questions for you to answer. Let me know if any of these things describe you. There is no penalty if something does not describe you, nor is there a reward if something does," she told him brusquely.

56

She began a verbal questionnaire that was similar to the one that he had answered in Sindra's office, although the statements focused on his feelings about being outside and studying plant and animal life.

Occasionally, she jotted down some notes as he answered, but for the most part, she merely watched him. She was deciding something about him. He could see an opinion forming behind her eyes, although he could not tell what that opinion was.

Something was peculiar about her steely, businesslike approach. He compared her to the Chancellor and Sindra and realized that *they* had both attempted to entice him to want to stay. This woman did not seem to care how he felt about staying at the school, and he wondered if she was used to working with new students. She had mentioned that she worked with ADVANCED STUDIES students, and he questioned why she had been told to speak with *him*.

As soon as her questions stopped, he bravely asked, "Is it unusual for you to conduct this kind of interview with a *transplant* on his very first day?"

He noted with interest that she did not ask him what a *transplant* was, which could mean that the faculty was aware that the *originals* bullied the new kids.

"Everett," she started and then paused as if to frame her response, "you are an enigma to us. We have little information about your background, your family, and your experiences outside of school. Your mother did not leave us with any information, and you are also unwilling to reveal information about yourself. The data that we *do* have from your schooling is not representative of your actual abilities because it appears that you concealed your considerable STRENGTHS from your teachers. Your advisor asked me to meet with you because she is concerned about you. You are in a place that welcomes learning, discovery, and risk-taking. If nature interests you, then we can build some learning opportunities into your routine that are more meaningful than a stroll through the Nature Center. Does that answer your question?"

Her stiff demeanor seemed to relax as she spoke, and by the end, her voice sounded almost kind. Everett felt that she might be more honest with him than the Chancellor and Sindra had been, so he risked another question.

"The students that I ate lunch with mentioned that the *originals'* parents are all G. How can *I* be gifted if my parents were not?" he asked.

She rocked back in her chair thoughtfully and then fixed him with her brown eyes.

"Are you certain that neither of your parents were gifted?" she asked.

Everett retreated from her gaze in confusion. He did not know anything about his father. On the few occasions that he had asked about him, his mother had been overcome by such intense grief and pain that he had decided to stop probing. She would only say that he could not be with them, but he would have been very proud of his son.

His thoughts turned to his mother. If she was a G, she would have the tattoo.

As he thought about what Greta had said about her family, he realized that their stories sounded similar. His mother had enriched his childhood with learning opportunities that had not been possible in his schooling, just like Greta's parents had with her.

A strange memory came to him. He remembered the day that Sindra had observed him creating patterns with pebbles on the play pad. When he had told his mother that the Observer had been a G, her hand had fluttered to her throat, right to the spot where Gs had their tattoo. This memory and the line of thinking that came with it disturbed him greatly, and he struggled to focus when he realized that Ms. Rosenthal had continued talking.

"....hereditary. A multitude of genes interplay to create a person's intelligence, personality, drives, and aptitudes. The NATURE side of understanding giftedness says that without these genes, no matter how enriched the environment, a person will not reach a gifted level of intelligence. However, the NURTURE side has shown that a child *with* these genes is often unable to fully express their POTENTIAL if they are not in an enriched environment. So yes, your gifted *POTENTIAL* does come from somewhere in your genetic history."

Everett allowed that to sink in and then pushed it to the back of his mind to process at a more private time. If his mother *was* a G, he had a lot of questions that he was not sure he would ever get the answer to.

"Thanks," he said casually, as if the information was not that important to him.

Her eyebrows created deep furrows in her forehead at his response, but she dismissed him to return to Sev. As he left, he admitted to himself that he had almost liked her odd but straightforward demeanor and wondered if he would get to see her again.

Exhaustion

Everett sagged against the wall when Sev told him that it was time for a mid-day meal break. Everything in his body screamed that it was time to go to his room, to process the day, and to have some time alone.

How could this only be the middle of the day?

Was their strategy to completely exhaust him into submission?

Sev read Everett's non-verbal cues and relayed a message to Sindra to request a period of solitude for his charge. The request was granted after a brief delay. Everett followed Sev back through the hallways to his room and gratefully collapsed onto his bed. The robot placed a meal order for Everett and retired to the corner to recharge once it arrived, sensing that Everett was not interested in conversing.

Everett remained face down on the bed for quite some time. It seemed impossible to him that he had ridden in a POD with his mother only yesterday, expecting to never see this place again. He rolled over as he thought about his day.

So far, he had gained some insight into the SENSUAL OVEREXCITABILITY and had learned that there were different definitions of giftedness *and* different ideas about the best way to educate gifted students.

He felt that he had made a friend in Greta and a great ally in Kimin. The only shadow over that success was the conflict that he had already experienced with the *originals*. He hoped that Kimin had been right that the hazing would end once his ORIENTATION was over.

Everett groaned aloud at this thought and pushed himself up to begin eating his meal.

Once his ORIENTATION was over!?

He wondered if he would even survive. It was only midway through his first day, and he felt completely overwhelmed and exhausted.

As he munched on his food, however, he remembered the debate that he had witnessed on his tour. His blood stirred as he remembered the fire in the students' eyes as they had laid out their points and the responding gleam in their opponents' eyes as they had countered. He also remembered the face of the instructor, who had been caught up in the debate and seemed to have no plans of calling the classroom to order so that the students would focus on him and hear his opinions.

As Everett placed his empty plate into the trash receptacle, he asked himself if he could ever go back to his previous school.

"Sev," he called out, feeling ready for the next step in his day.

The robot jolted out of sleep mode and seemed slightly disoriented as he asked, "What are your needs at the moment?"

Everett concealed a sympathetic grin at the robot's confusion as he asked Sev to plug into the terminal to see where he needed to go next. If it was possible, Sev seemed indignant at the suggestion and quickly relayed that they would be heading back to Mr. Dodd's classroom *without* using the terminal.

Everett had felt comfortable with Mr. Dodd, and his steps quickened as they got closer. As he entered the classroom, Kimin playfully scolded him for not joining them for the afternoon meal, while Greta sent him a sympathetic smile to show that she understood.

He could not believe that his feelings about the school had changed so quickly. That morning he had felt angry, disjointed, and pessimistic, but he was amazed to realize that he now felt a partial sense of belonging and an excitement for what they would discuss next.

Mr. Dodd swept into the room with a big smile on his face as he brushed a few crumbs off of his generous stomach. He walked to the board at the front of the room and drew a giant question mark on it with great flourish.

Everett noted that the other students pressed forward in their chairs with excitement. He was surprised to see that even Greta had a goofy grin on her face.

Seeing his dumbfounded expression, she leaned over to whisper, "When Mr. Dodd puts up the question mark, we can ask him questions about *anything,* and he has to answer!"

Everett smiled in anticipation.

Mr. Dodd sat in a chair in the center of the room and waited expectantly with his arms crossed over his chest.

"What did you have for your meal today?" Sonniy asked with a giggle as she eyed the remaining crumbs on his shirt.

"A carrot-apple muffin," Mr. Dodd replied with a smile that caused a crinkle to appear around his eyes.

"Yum!" Kimin and Sonniy said in unison and then broke into giggles.

The students asked a few more playful questions, including inquiries about his health, books that he was reading, pet names, and other personal questions. Kimin turned the game more serious with her first question.

"We were talking about giftedness running in families today. If giftedness is just inherited from our families, why did we have to take a test? What about the kids that attend the SFGP that never took a test? Are they really gifted if there is no proof?" she asked.

Mr. Dodd shifted in his chair with a thoughtful expression on his face.

"It is interesting that you say *proof*," he replied. "You all took a variety of tests with the Evaluators when you arrived here. The GENERAL INTELLECTUAL ABILITY tests that you were given evaluated your reasoning skills, vocabulary, memory, and thinking skills."

Everett thought back to the tests that he had taken. It had been easy to fake his answers on the pencil and paper tests, but he had also taken oral tests that had asked him questions about word meanings, information about a variety of topics, and had tested his memory by giving him information early in the test and asking him about it later. The Evaluator had given him some pieces of information and then had encouraged him to use that information in new ways, to apply the information to unrelated concepts, and to create new ideas from the information given.

It had been difficult to give the wrong answers on those tests because he had enjoyed the intellectual exercise.

"You were also given tests to uncover your SPECIFIC ACADEMIC APTITUDES. Those tests were looking for outstanding achievement in reading or math. Your RESULTS on those tests will determine which classes you are placed in once your ORIENTATION is complete," Mr. Dodd continued.

Everett suddenly wished that he had tried harder on his tests. Of course, he had not known that his mother was going to leave him, but now that she had, he found that he wanted to know about his STRENGTHS and weaknesses.

"In addition, however, we have extensive behavioral data that has been collected on you for years. Any child of a G is watched from birth in order to look for signs of giftedness. We use observations of your behavior, interests, reasoning ability, vocabulary... the list is extensive. Students are not accepted to the SFGP based on just one piece of data. We also look for these behaviors in children that are *not* from families with a documented history of giftedness and ask teachers to contact us if they find a student that displays gifted CHARACTERISTICS. As for the children that come to our school as infants, these behaviors *are* observed and documented very carefully by the instructors here. Although they may not know it, they have all been tested at various points in their lives, just as you were, for intellectual ability and academic aptitudes. The "proof" comes from everything that you say and do, and your testing only gave us a few pieces to the puzzle that makes *you* who you are," Mr. Dodd finished.

The "proof" comes from everything that you say and do, echoed in Everett's mind.

Now I understand why I confused Sindra and the Evaluators so much, he thought wryly. Somehow his mother had known exactly what the Observers would be watching for and had coached him to show the opposite behaviors.

Sonniy frowned and crossed her arms defensively as she shared, "I haven't made connections with *any* of the OEs that we've talked about yet. The Evaluators told my parents that I show gifted POTENTIAL in the areas of math and PERFORMING ARTS. Not having an OE is making me feel like I'm not supposed to be here."

"I want to remind you that giftedness is not directly related to the OVEREXCITABILITIES," Mr. Dodd said. "Not all gifted people have them and having one or many OEs does not make you gifted. Some of the OEs are found in the general population and these traits have been *applied* to highly gifted people, but are not exclusive to them. The OEs are one component of a developmental POTENTIAL that can lead to an advanced development for some people. The OEs and the CHARACTERISTICS of gifted people are pieces of the puzzle that make you the person that you are. As we learn about the gifted CHARACTERISTICS, you should not expect to have them *all*. Your journey at this school is about *discovering* your POTENTIAL just as much as it is about developing it."

Sonniy sniffed and raised her chin slightly.

"You can show LEADERSHIP qualities, the CREATIVE THINKING ABILITY, and the INTELLECTUAL OE, while the kid next to you might demonstrate a SPECIFIC ACADEMIC APTITUDE in math and experience the PSYCHOMOTOR OE," Mr. Dodd continued. "Both of you are gifted, but you each have different interests and STRENGTHS. Giftedness can be a difficult thing to define and different cultures have had different definitions of it at different times. It is important to understand *yourself* and what makes you who you are. That goes beyond a test score or your answers on a questionnaire."

Jeremiah cleared his throat awkwardly.

"Does everyone at this school have a STRENGTH in everything? Do gifted people not have any weaknesses?" he asked, his voice cracking slightly.

Mr. Dodd shook his head as he answered, "That is a common misconception Jeremiah. You all have a STRENGTH, but you may also have a weakness or several weaknesses. Some gifted people have a weakness that is just as extreme as their STRENGTH."

Kimin sat up on her knees as she said, "I don't understand. Do you mean that someone can be really good at math but not know how to read?"

Mr. Dodd smiled as he answered, "Sometimes there is an extreme difference in SPECIFIC ACADEMIC APTITUDES, like reading and math, but a gifted person can also be challenged with an emotional or social need as well. The important thing to remember is that, no matter what your challenges are, our school is dedicated to helping you reach your full POTENTIAL in *all* areas. We will celebrate and educate every aspect of you; STRENGTHS, weaknesses, and everything in between."

A tear slipped down Jeremiah's cheek at these words, and Mr. Dodd patted him encouragingly on the back as he got up to erase the question mark.

Some of the students groaned playfully because the activity was over, and a few turned to each other to discuss what they had heard. Everett peeked at the instructor, who was rummaging through a bag on his desk, and wondered nervously if Mr. Dodd would scold them for chatting.

Greta took the pressure away from him when she scooted her chair next to him. He wished that he could open up to Greta the same way that she had with him, but he had been guarded for so long that he did not know how. She patiently waited for him to speak as he struggled to find the words to start a conversation, but they sat in silence for quite a while. She gave him a regretful smile and a reassuring squeeze on the arm when she realized that he was not going to share anything and slid her chair over to where Kimin, Sonniy, and Jeremiah were talking.

Kimin's sweet face twisted into a sympathetic frown as she bobbed her head to the story that Jeremiah was sharing. He seemed distraught by whatever memory he was recollecting and was even slightly tearful. Everett wished for such abandon, but it was still too soon for him to share such intimate details with these strangers, even if they were accepting and kind.

Mr. Dodd shuffled around the room and handed each student a slim, silver rectangle. He announced something to the class before he dismissed them to their next activity, but Everett had been distracted by Jeremiah and did not hear what his instructor had said.

Everett panicked when he saw that Kimin, Sonniy, Greta, and Jeremiah had already headed into the hallway together without a backwards glance for him. They were still listening to Jeremiah share his story and were all providing feedback at the same time.

He realized that he did not know what to do with the object in his hands, but feared that he would get in trouble if he asked Mr. Dodd. Sev answered his unspoken question by opening his mid-section to reveal a small screen that played a recording of Mr. Dodd's instructions about what to do with the silver rectangle.

Everett had forgotten that Sev was recording his classes. The video showed that the rectangle contained an assignment that had to be completed that evening. Sev placed the object in a protective pouch and told Everett that he would teach him how to use it after dinner. Relieved, Everett hurried into the hallway to catch his friends before they left.

To his disappointment, he did not see them in the hallway, but he did see Sindra walking toward him. He groaned aloud, although he did not realize that it had been out loud until he saw the piqued look on her face.

"Good afternoon Everett. I thought that I would check in with you before I left to go home because of the rough start that you had today. Please join me for a refreshment," she said in a way that was not really a request.

She turned on her heel and retraced her steps, not even looking back to see if he was following. It took a slight prod from Sev to make Everett move, and he sullenly followed his advisor. His robot had said that the next activity was recreational time, and he was looking forward to going back to the Nature Center.

Sindra remained a few steps ahead of him the entire way. It had been a difficult day. Although she had planned to leave early, the Chancellor had requested that she look into Everett's CNI data to build a more complete profile of him. She had spent the majority of her day digging into Everett's past but had found nothing beyond school attendance, medical, and dental records. She still did not have a sense of who he was and knew even less about his mother.

She intended to get more information from Everett immediately.

He sat morosely at a table in the nearly empty room and rejected the light snack that she brought him. His face was a dark cloud of irritation and annoyance, and it did not improve Sindra's mood.

"I am here to collect information about you and your mother," Sindra said as she grabbed her CNIpad and logged in.

He maintained a pointed silence. She allowed the time to tick by slowly, although her irritation was growing.

She recognized that he could win this battle because she had no leverage, and the petty thought of keeping him until his recreational time was over crossed her mind. Sindra knew that she was being immature and silently scolded herself for being unprofessional.

Admitting defeat, she slowly logged off of her CNIpad and tucked it away.

Her voice was clipped but polite as she instructed Sev to take Everett to join his classmates. She watched the boy stand up and turn slowly on his heel to follow his robot.

He did not give her a backwards glance.

It was good that he did not, because he would have seen Sindra looking tired, hurt, and defeated. For now, he needed Sindra to be a strong opponent.

Friendship

Everett walked quickly into the rec center and hoped to find Greta in the Nature Center. He was anxious to escape into its humid serenity. Unfortunately, he saw Greta, Sonniy, and Kimin clustered around Jeremiah at the edge of a court of some kind.

Everett wondered if he *had* to go over to the group. He had never belonged to a social group before, and he wondered if they would be upset with him for not joining them, even though he needed to use this time to recharge in the Nature Center.

He hung indecisively in the doorway as his eyes flicked between his friends and the outdoor enclosure. As she had done several times before, Greta gave him the answer that he needed. She caught his eye and motioned for him to go to the Nature Center, then smiled and nodded to reassure him that it was okay.

A smile of relief cracked his face so unexpectedly that it almost hurt.

Relief washed over him as he entered the enclosure. He stood in the entrance with his eyes closed and his mouth open as his senses absorbed his surroundings. He took in the dense, humid air as his ears filled with the sounds of animals rustling, birds chirping, and the distant sound of running water. Finally, he opened his eyes and found a creek that was flowing south and headed north to find its source.

Everett was observing the fish in a shallow pond as they darted through the shimmering water when he felt a presence at his elbow. He turned and saw with relief that it was Greta. They exchanged a smile as Greta smoothed her skirt behind her knees so that she could squat to observe the fish.

"This school has a huge facility where they research the plants and animals of all of the regions on Earth. They rotate a new biome into the Nature Center every two months. The South American rain forest is on display right now," she said softly.

Everett smiled in response. He did not really feel like talking, but he enjoyed Greta's company. She took his silence as a request for solitude and started to get up. He grabbed her wrist softly and pulled her back down. Understanding crossed her face, and she settled next to him to observe the animals and plants in the pond.

They spent the rest of their recreational period happily immersed in their own study of the natural world and at ease in each other's company. A soft gong signaled the end of the recreational period, and the pair exchanged a regretful smile as they got up and moved toward the door.

They met up with their friends at the entrance. Kimin explained that the students in the ORIENTATION phase were now dismissed to go back to their dormitories, while the other students had another class, usually one that they chose from an area of interest.

"But everyone must be interested in so many different things. How can they offer that many classes?" Sonniy asked.

"From what I heard, the instructors try to *facilitate* student learning in an area of interest. They teach you *how* to learn so that everyone can focus on different topics," Kimin replied with a shrug.

Everett found himself intrigued yet again. With all of his interests, where would he start?

He followed Sev back to his room with his mind in a whirlwind and his body in need of rest. When he had made the same walk to his room the night before, feeling betrayed and uneasy, he could not have anticipated that he would be feeling this way now. He was overwhelmed, but exhilarated, and strangely felt as though he belonged. After only a day!

He ran a shower for himself while Sev placed his meal order. The steaming water covered his tired, sore muscles as he thought about Greta, Kimin, Sonniy, and Jeremiah.

Friends!

Interesting and complex friends.

People around his own age that he could identify with.

He had been able to talk with them, had understood their feelings, and had connected with their life experiences. A wave of excitement coursed through him and a chill crossed his body despite the hot water.

As he stepped out of the shower, he smelled that his dinner had arrived and dressed quickly. He eagerly dug into his dish and asked Sev to show him what was on the disk that Mr. Dodd had sent him around a mouthful of carrots.

Mr. Dodd's face appeared on the panel on Everett's wall. It was a video message especially for Everett.

"Good evening Everett. I hope that you took some time to relax and refocus before you asked your robot to turn on this video. The first day at The School for Gifted Potentials can be both exhilarating and exhausting. If you feel that you need additional time to rest before continuing this activity, please ask your robot to pause the video at this time."

Mr. Dodd paused to allow Everett to think about his needs. Everett surprised himself when he shook his head at Sev to show that he wanted to delve into his first independent assignment immediately.

"Let's begin," Mr. Dodd said after a pause. "We use something called a *brain bridge* to learn at our school. A brain bridge helps you diagram or sketch your ideas, the connections that you have made, and compose questions that you want to ask the following day. Robot Number Seventeen, please give Everett his SKEtch pad."

The video had another lengthy pause.

During the pause, Sev reached into his inner compartment and pulled out a paper-thin 14x16 rectangle. It had a screen and a stylus to write with. Everett grasped the novel item with excitement.

The SKEtch pad flashed on as the heat of his hands touched it. His name slowly formed in gold letters in the center of the screen and then faded. He felt a tingle of excitement as he lifted the slim metal stylus and touched it gently to the face of the screen.

Mr. Dodd's voice directed him to touch the symbol shaped like a cogwheel in the upper right corner. Everett had never had access to this kind of technology before but instantly felt at ease with the process. He touched the cogwheel symbol and the small wheel zoomed forward to form a larger wheel in the center of the screen. Each cog was now labeled with a space for a word.

Mr. Dodd directed him to tap the word *bridge* and then instructed him to look back at the screen. Mr. Dodd held a similar pad in his hands and had already created a partial bridge. The word *carrot-apple muffin* was in the center of his bridge. Everett smiled as he recalled the game that they had played in the classroom that day. Several bridges radiated out from the word that had ideas about the topic connected to it. One was labeled *taste*, one was labeled *cooking process*, and another was labeled *experiences*.

Mr. Dodd showed him the menu of options in the left corner. He used the stylus to highlight the word *experiences* and then tapped an icon shaped like a looking glass.

The original bridge zoomed away and only the word *experiences* remained. Mr. Dodd showed him how to use the arrow tool from the menu to connect words and ideas to the central word. As an example,

71

he connected *today's lunch* to the center word and then highlighted it with the stylus and tapped the looking glass.

Again, the bridge zoomed away and he was left with *today's lunch*. He moved that word to the top and sketched a picture of himself eating the muffin.

Mr. Dodd explained that he could write sentences and paragraphs, draw pictures, and record his voice to add to a bridge. Once he had demonstrated each of these options, he explained the assignment.

"Use these tools to compile what you learned today. This will be saved in your personal database for future reference. I look forward to seeing you tomorrow."

Mr. Dodd flashed a sincere smile as the video stopped.

Everett hardly noticed. He had already written *first day* as the topic before Mr. Dodd's face had faded from the screen.

He bridged several sub-categories to the center word; *friends, advisor, tour, classes, new understandings,* and *originals.* He paused after reviewing the list, unsure of which sub-category to start with. As his eyes scanned the screen, he realized that all of the topics were difficult to begin with because they were all linked to his jumble of emotions.

He got up to pace his room because he did not know how to sort through those feelings. *Friends* seemed like an easy place to start, but he had never had real friends before, and he wasn't quite sure what to call what he was feeling about them. He definitely felt anger and frustration about the *originals,* excitement and curiosity about his *classes,* irritation with his *advisor,* confusion about the brief *tour,* and intrigued by his *new understandings.*

Shrugging, he decided that labeling those emotions was a good enough start and quickly added them as descriptors under each sub-topic. He then went back to *friends,* savoring the word, and quickly added the names Kimin and Greta. He considered putting Sonniy and Jeremiah but decided that he really had not developed a friendship with them yet. He wanted to describe Kimin and Greta, especially Greta, but could not find the words that he needed.

Vocabulary was rarely a problem for Everett, but he had also never been asked to describe two girls that were his friends before either.

A soft ringing that came from a panel on the wall near his bed startled Everett. He looked at Sev, who had unfortunately gone into sleep mode. While he was deciding whether to wake the robot, he noticed an *accept* button on the panel. When he pushed it, Kimin's giggling face popped up on his screen.

"I just wanted to say good night Everett! I hope that you had a great first day, and I am so glad that we are friends. Don't stay up too late. Tomorrow will feel even longer than today did- *trust* me!" Kimin ended with an exaggerated wink and another giggle before her image disappeared.

An uncontrollable grin spread across Everett's face. He now knew exactly what to say about Kimin! Just as he was about to pick up the stylus, he heard another ring. He pushed the *accept* button eagerly and was excited to see Greta's face.

"Hi Everett... this is just a video message from me to you... to say good night. I am glad that you are here." Greta's face flushed red before the screen went black.

Heat spread across Everett's face, along with a goofy grin that he could not quite get rid of.

He picked up the stylus and activated the screen, buzzing with nervous excitement. Under *Kimin* he wrote *kind, observant, effervescent, gregarious, ally.* He added a quick sketch of her face and a pair of binoculars to remind himself that while she played the part of a silly, giggling girl, she also played the role of a secret spy, free to watch and learn about others because they dismissed her so easily.

He tapped Greta's name and paused. He struggled to find the words that he wanted to use to describe the first child that he had ever truly connected with. After a moment of hesitation, under her name he simply drew a treasure box, partially opened.

With a soft smile, he turned off the screen and dropped into bed, too exhausted to dream.

Attacked

Everett awoke the next morning to an agitated robot. A plate of breakfast food was already on the table, and his clothes were laid out next to him. Sleepily, he wished the robot a good morning.

"I apologize for making your meal selection for you. You have overslept and might be late to meet with your advisor. Please eat and dress quickly," Sev said brusquely.

Everett was still amazed at how many human emotions the robot was able to display. He ate his breakfast rapidly and started dressing with his mouth still full of the last bite. He almost spit it out with laughter when the robot's face contorted into something that looked like disgust.

The robot ushered him out of his room as he was still buttoning his shirt. He was fully dressed by the time they arrived at Sindra's door, and Sev admitted that he was a minute early. When Sindra's door panel slid open, Everett entered and took a seat in his chair. He did not realize it, but he looked relaxed and confident, and Sindra chose not to point it out.

"Good morning Everett," she said kindly.

He noticed that she was in the process of hanging up a poster of the first humans landing on Mars. He had poured through the books that were available about the recent lunar and planetary landings. The space program had gone to private funding sources several decades before and had exploded. New findings were reported almost daily about what astronauts and scientists were discovering.

Sindra smoothed her skirt as she sat down and paused briefly to enjoy the interested look on his handsome face as he studied the poster.

"Are you interested in space exploration?" she asked.

For once, she sounded genuinely interested, not as if she was just searching for an item to put in his file.

"Yeah," he replied noncommittally as he flicked his gaze away from the poster to look out of the window. "They landed on Mars for the first time the year that I was born."

"That's right. Two of the astronauts were students at this school," she replied.

"Really?" he asked and sat up in eagerly in his chair. "I never knew that. Is it possible to meet them sometime?"

Sindra smiled and said, "I can see if that could be arranged. One of the astronauts, Landon Perry, is a personal friend of the Chancellor."

Everett leaned back and put his disinterested face back on, but *inside* he was excited. His mother had been very interested in the recent activity in space. Thinking back, he realized that she had paid special attention to the INTELLEX crew, which Landon Perry was a part of.

"Mr. Dodd and Mr. Elan told me that you connected with the SENSUAL OVEREXCITABILITY. I also found out that you are interested in nature. Do you have any thoughts about these topics that you'd like to share?" she asked.

Everett paused. A small part of him wanted to continue being antagonistic toward his advisor, but a larger part wanted answers.

"Well, I have always been frustrated by being able to hear every little sound, and I have wished before that I could tune out irritating sounds like other people. When we discussed the SENSUAL OVEREXCITABILITY though, I realized that there is a positive side to my reaction to sounds that I had never thought about before. Another kid said that he reacts to music with intense joy, which made me realize that part of what I *enjoy* about nature is all of the sounds that I can hear. I love the sounds of rustling leaves, and rushing water, and the whirring of insect wings. I guess I never realized that enjoying some sounds so much could be related to being irritated by other sounds," he mused.

Sindra nodded encouragingly.

"I am also constantly touching things because I like different textures," he continued. "Mr. Dodd explained that I am more *aware* of what I'm feeling and can have a *range* of reactions to what I experience, which explains why I also dislike certain sensations, like hair on my forehead."

A long pause stretched between them, and he could tell that she wanted more information about his first day. The discussion with Mr. Dodd the day before about "proof" had weighed heavily on his mind. His classmates seemed to know so much about their STRENGTHS, but he had learned very little from his discussion with the Chancellor.

Taking a deep breath he said, "I guess I would like to know what my test results were. We talked about the GENERAL INTELLECTUAL ABILITY and SPECIFIC ACADEMIC APTITUDES in Mr. Dodd's class yesterday, and I want to know if I have any STRENGTHS in those areas."

Confusion over his question stopped Sindra for a moment. Each child tested at the SFGP was given an extensive amount of information about their RESULTS before they were accepted into the school. It was strange that Everett seemed to have no knowledge of his STRENGTHS. What else would have been discussed at his RESULTS session?

A foreboding chill crept down her spine as she logged into her CNIpad.

"I am pulling up your RESULTS right now. It will only take a moment," she said, smiling reassuringly at him as she pulled up his file. "All right. I will do my best to explain this, as I do not usually interpret test scores. According to your data, it appears that you have been categorized as highly gifted based on the data from your GENERAL INTELLECTUAL ABILITY tests. You also show SPECIFIC ACADEMIC APTITUDES in the areas of math and reading. Other STRENGTHS may be added once you demonstrate advanced POTENTIAL in your classes and electives."

A strange knot formed in his stomach as he heard the RESULTS. Although it felt good to know more about himself, it was also disconcerting to find out that he truly did belong at the school.

She waited for a few moments as he processed the information and then prodded him to say more about his first day.

"I guess the best part of my first day was that I learned that I can make friends and that I share a lot of qualities with some of the kids in my classes," he continued after a moment of thought.

Sindra looked somewhat smug and triumphant at his words, and he regretted that he had given her so many positive comments about his first day.

Hoping to take back his control of the situation, he added, "I also found out that the *originals* are a group of kids that have attended this school since they were infants and that they enjoy belittling the new kids."

Sindra's self-satisfied grin faded at this last piece of information, and she shuffled a few papers on her desk before she spoke.

"Well, I gather that you had a full day and that you understand yourself a little better. I hope that today is just as fruitful. Number Seventeen has your itinerary and is ready to take you to your first class," she said with false brightness.

Sindra turned her back to Everett and waited for him to leave. He paused, wanting to goad her into responding to the information he had given her about the *originals*, and then stalked out of her office.

Everett's steps quickened as he got closer to Mr. Dodd's class. There were more OVEREXCITABILITIES to learn about, and he could not wait to know more.

His ears picked up the sound of crying, and he followed the sound to a corner of the hallway. Jeremiah was hunched against the wall with his long legs pulled awkwardly up to his chest. Tears rolled down his pockmarked face as he wiped his nose on his sleeve. Everett's chest seized up with anger and worry.

He crouched by Jeremiah's side feeling uncomfortable and uncertain. Would the other boy want to have privacy in this moment or an ally?

His answer came when Jeremiah's bony hand gripped his upper arm. He used Everett to pull himself up off of the floor.

Everett stood up as well. Not knowing what else to say, he asked, "Where is your robot?"

Jeremiah snuffled and wiped his nose on his other sleeve.

"I left him in my room today. I thought that if I didn't have a robot with me..." Jeremiah replied.

Everett caught his meaning immediately.

"Do you mean that an *original* did something to you?" he asked.

Jeremiah nodded and was about to say something more when Mr. Dodd appeared in the hallway to search for his missing students. Everett moved forward to get Mr. Dodd's help with the situation.

Jeremiah gripped his arm almost painfully and pleaded, "Don't tell anyone, okay?"

Against his better judgment, Everett agreed with a curt nod of his head and then pulled his arm out of the other boy's grasp. He brushed past Mr. Dodd, who watched him curiously, and sank glumly into the chair next to Greta. He refused to make eye contact with her or Kimin so that they would not see the anger and frustration that was firing in his eyes. Mr. Dodd stayed out in the hallway for quite some time to speak with Jeremiah.

Once he had calmed down enough to act indifferent, he turned to look at his friends. Kimin looked angry and Greta looked hurt.

He swallowed hard, not wanting to alienate his friends, and whispered, "I'll tell you later."

Kimin, always perceptive, flicked her eyes between Everett and Jeremiah, who was now walking into the classroom, and seemed to understand what he meant. Greta, on the other hand, calmly got up and crossed to a seat next to Sonniy. She did not make eye contact with Everett. A new frustration boiled inside of him when he saw her demeanor, and he hoped that she would forgive him for shutting her out.

As he looked across the room at Greta, Everett noticed a new student. He looked a little older than Everett and was strikingly handsome with dark blond hair and an athletic frame. His bright blue eyes sparkled with confidence. Everett wondered if the boy's confidence would be a positive quality or if it would make him arrogant like the *original* that had tripped Everett in the hallway the day before.

Everett's gaze flicked briefly to Kimin to see if she had noticed the newcomer. Of course, she had, and because Mr. Dodd was still preoccupied, she pulled the stranger out of his seat and over to Everett's chair.

With the boy looming over Everett's chair, Kimin said, "Everett, this is Kabe. Kabe, this is Everett."

Everett felt self-conscious sitting in his chair while the others stood over him, so he jumped up and offered his hand to Kabe. The other boy's firm handshake surprised him. Kimin pranced away to sit by Sonniy and Greta and left the two boys standing awkwardly together.

"So, what is your robot's number?" Everett asked, unable to think of a better question.

"Number Twelve," Kabe responded, looking unsure about the nature of the question.

"Oh, my robot's number is seventeen," Everett replied lamely.

Kabe nodded and looked around the room as if he was not sure how to follow that question with more conversation. Everett did not know what else to say either. They were saved when Mr. Dodd ambled toward the group and beckoned the chatting children to circle around him for a discussion. By the time that Kabe and Everett reached the circle, they had to sit next to each other because the other seats were taken.

"Good morning to you all. We have a new student with us today. Kabe, we discuss the CHARACTERISTICS of gifted learners and the OVEREXCITABILITIES in this class. I will chat with you soon to catch you up. Today we will discuss the EMOTIONAL OVEREXCITABILITY. This is a complex OVEREXCITABILITY, and you will learn some managing strategies for it with Mr. Elan later today," Mr. Dodd assured them.

Everett and Greta exchanged a look as they each wondered what they would be discussing.

"People with the EMOTIONAL OE tend to experience emotions more *intensely* than other people, have a greater *range* of emotions, and can be more *aware* of their emotions. Your emotions will be *felt* more deeply," Mr. Dodd said as his gaze flicked to Jeremiah, who still had a myriad of emotions playing across his face. "People with this OE can make deep emotional attachments to other people, places, and things. Your first week here may be difficult because you have lost some relationships that were deeply valuable to you."

Everett's deep attachment to his mother was enough to convince him that he had this OVEREXCITABILITY. His whole life, he had felt connected to her in every thought and feeling, and despite his conflicting feelings about her abandonment, he still missed her deeply.

"Let's think about the *intensity* of your emotions. A child that enters this school *without* this OE may feel a sense of loss and sadness over losing their family, while a child *with* the OE may describe their feelings as crushing grief or intense sorrow," Mr. Dodd explained.

Greta wiped away a silent tear as she related to Mr. Dodd's words.

"With this OE, you will be more *aware* of your feelings than most. You may find that you have intense reactions to your perception of how others treat you, feel about you, and react to you. Be aware that you might also be overly critical of yourself," Mr. Dodd said and then paused for emphasis. "Please collect your SKEtch pad from your robots."

Everett had been so focused on what Mr. Dodd was saying that the movement of the other students startled him. The robots in the room were suddenly active and the sound of whirring tracks filled the room. Everett was stressed by the commotion and his lack of understanding of what he was supposed to collect.

What was a SKEtch pad?

His faithful robot had already pulled out the silver screen with the stylus that Everett had used to do his assignment the night before and was moving to Everett to give it to him. As Sev approached, Everett's stomach dropped as he remembered what he had written about his friends the night before. Would they be able to see it when he turned the SKEtch pad on? His stomach twisted painfully at the thought of Greta seeing the treasure box associated with her name.

He scooted his chair away from the circle so that no one could look at his SKEtch pad and was annoyed when Kabe rocked his chair back to look at Everett's screen. Embarrassed, Everett jerked his screen toward his chest so that the other boy could not see it.

Kabe put his chair back on the floor and looked away. Everett felt bad for being rude, especially when he noticed that nothing that he had written the night before was on his screen.

Once Kabe had received his SKEtch pad from his robot, Everett leaned forward to tell him how to use the stylus, hoping to make amends. Mr. Dodd scanned the room to make sure that everyone had activated their screens and then shared a tip that a shield could pop up out of the top of the unit with a press of a button, which could be used to ensure that no one was able to see the screen.

Kabe activated his shield and then turned his chair slightly so that it blocked Everett's line of sight. Everett was irritated until he realized that he had acted the same way with Kabe.

"There are many *wonderful* emotions that you will feel on a deep, intense level with this OE. Because of the range of this OE, however, you will also experience some negative emotions more intensely as well. You may also experience a physical reaction to an emotion, such as nausea, muscle tension, crying, uncontrollable laughter, or skin coloration. Your emotional memory allows you to remember your feelings longer and with more intensity than others. For example, recalling a moment when you were embarrassed, even if it is years later, might bring on a gut wrenching reaction as you recall the incident," Mr. Dodd continued.

81

Jeremiah sniffed and got up to wipe his nose. Everett was not sure if he was reacting to an older memory or if he was still trying to get over what had happened to him in the hallway.

Mr. Dodd patted Jeremiah's shoulder as he continued, "I would like for you to think about a time that you had a *physical reaction* to an emotion. You should also think about how the *memory* of an emotion that you felt may still be intense to experience, even if a great amount of time has passed. Make some notes or drawings about any connections that you have made with this OE. If you are unable to connect to this OE, you may sketch or write about anything that you feel inclined to at this time."

Everett watched Mr. Dodd pull Kabe aside and then tapped the cog symbol and the bridge icon. He wrote EMOTIONAL OE in the center of the screen and created the sub-categories *intensity of emotion, physical reactions,* and *emotional memory.* His mind raced with a multitude of connections.

He tapped *physical reactions* and wrote out *blushing, stomachache, headaches, muscle aches, nausea, chills,* and *jaw tightening.* Each described a physical reaction that he had felt in reaction to emotions like anger, embarrassment, frustration, and nervousness. He also experienced some of those reactions when he felt excitement, anticipation, and even love. Thoughts of love brought up thoughts of his mother, and a pain started in his stomach that radiated out through his body.

To escape from this reaction, he looked around the room and noted that Greta, Kimin, and Jeremiah were busy adding information to their SKEtch pads, while Kabe and Sonniy seemed to be sketching for pleasure. He took that to mean that they were not making connections with the EMOTIONAL OE.

He felt composed again and selected *emotional memory* from the main screen. Under that category, he put a few key words to describe several memories that still caused a physical reaction when he thought of them.

For his worst memories, he wrote The School for Gifted Potentials. His stomach still dropped when he thought back to the day that he had told his mother about the Observer noticing his activity on the play pad. He also recalled the sick feeling that he had gotten when the letter requiring him to test had arrived, and the terrible feeling that he still felt when he recalled the Chancellor's words, *"Your mother*

82

has specifically requested that you be accepted here. Her request overrides the need for your acceptance. Because of this, you do not have a choice in the matter."

The memory of this incident was still so fresh and distressing to Everett that he had to force himself to draw a long, deep breath. He held it in tightly until the sensation of his chest bursting for air overrode the sensation of pain in his stomach, and then loudly pushed the air out of his lungs. He felt more relaxed afterward, even though he was embarrassed by the looks that he got from the others.

Greta's concerned eyes lingered on him for a few moments longer than the others, which Everett took as a possible sign that they were on speaking terms again.

Everett grabbed his stylus and added a new bridge that he called *connections*. He drew a short line and labeled one end *happy* and the other end *sad*. Beside it, he drew another, much longer line, which went way past the first line on either end. He labeled the ends of the longer line *rapture* and *despair* to represent that his emotions had a greater range and depth than other people.

Next, he drew a stick figure facing three other stick figures. Then he drew an arrow from the eyes of his stick figure to the faces of the other stick figures to remind himself that he was more aware of how other people reacted to him. He added a question mark over his head to show that he was always thinking about what other people thought of him.

Finally, he drew another picture of himself with a frowning face and an X over the picture to warn himself to not be so critical of himself.

As he stood up to stretch, he noticed that he was not the only one that was having a difficult time making it through the process. Greta and Jeremiah had pained looks on their faces, and Kimin scowled as she rapidly wrote something on her screen.

Mr. Dodd must have sensed how emotionally charged the classroom had become because he instructed the robots to retrieve the SKEtch pads and gave the students the last few minutes of class to walk around and release some of their energy and tension.

Everett moved to Greta's side and she shot him a smile that told him that she was no longer mad. Kabe had moved to Greta's side as well and had engaged her in a conversation about the features of the SKEtch pad. Everett hovered at the edge of the pair and tried to look interested in what they were saying and pretend that he was a part of the conversation, but felt uncomfortable when he was not included.

He moved away from them and asked Sev if he could go a few minutes early. Sev quickly asked Mr. Dodd for permission. He looked quizzically at Everett but nodded and gestured to the door. Everett silently followed Sev out of the classroom with his hands in his pockets and his head hung low.

The Photograph

His mood began to improve as he followed Sev across another sky bridge to go on a tour of a science wing. Everett sped up as the smell of animals, plants, and decaying matter filled his nostrils. He almost passed Sev but slowed down when he realized that he did not know where he was supposed to go.

"Yesterday you started a tour of the Arts Wing," Sev began. "Today you will tour the Life and Natural Sciences Wing. This wing was added fourteen years ago. Before this wing was added, the students working on a MASTERY project in Natural Sciences had to study away from the school, in natural places, which meant that they had little support from instructors and fewer MASTERY students to collaborate with. It was also difficult to conduct experiments because it is challenging to create a controlled environment in nature. Five students wrote a petition to the Board of the school to ask for the opportunity to study plants and animals *at* The School for Gifted Potentials. They argued that all of the other MASTERY students had a wing or a complex that housed the staff and the equipment that they needed to pursue advanced learning opportunities. The students helped design the entire facility and were there for the groundbreaking. Their original vision has continued to grow, and this is now a truly impressive facility."

Sev paused briefly to show Everett a photograph of the students that had written the petition. It had been taken at the groundbreaking ceremony and was a candid of the group. He was startled to notice the handsome young face of Landon Perry in the photo. His dark hair hung down over his forehead, and his brown eyes gleamed with pride. Everett was curious to know why Landon had switched gears from studying plants and animals to train to become an astronaut. For some reason, Everett felt drawn to Landon Perry and wanted to know more about his history.

Sev rolled away and Everett turned to follow him, until the image of the young woman that held tightly to Landon's arm caught his eye. Her face was mostly covered by her long, dark hair, but there was something familiar about her profile that tugged at his mind.

He wanted to spend more time studying the picture, but Sev had already turned to remind Everett that they had a limited amount of time and a lot to see. Reluctantly, Everett turned away from the photograph and told himself that he would see it again when they passed through the hallway on their way back.

The rest of Everett's tour was absolute bliss. He observed a wide variety of scientific experiments and observations that were occurring in reproductions of Earth's major biomes. There was even a deep sea simulator that allowed several scientists and their MASTERY students to study the adaptive characteristics of the flora and fauna that thrived there. The development of the simulator had helped scientists develop a greater understanding of the adaptations of the life forms that lived in the deep trenches of the sea, just inches from the molten crust. The scientists were using their new understandings of these organisms to create advancements in medicine, transportation, and construction.

The replica of an African rainforest was the most impressive portion of the facility. The trees towered overhead, and the glass panels that enclosed the space were so high overhead that he had to trust Sev that they were even there.

Everett almost laughed out loud when he thought, *they should have just brought me* here *on the first day.*

As they left the facility, Everett bombarded Sev with questions. Some of the answers were programmed into the robot's database, but many were not, and Sev promised to send the questions on to Ms. Rosenthal. Everett was so engaged in questioning Sev that he did not realize that they had passed Landon Perry's photograph until they were already across the sky bridge. He asked Sev to take him back to it, but the robot refused to turn around.

Sev ushered Everett to the refreshment area where he entered his food and beverage request as if it was second nature. His friends were already seated, and he watched them from across the room for a moment.

As usual, Kimin gregariously dominated the conversation while Sonniy hung on her every word. Kabe was leaning back in his chair with his arms crossed over his chest. He was smiling at Kimin's words but was also scanning the room to look at the other students.

Greta sat next to Kabe. Her body politely faced Kimin, but her face showed that her thoughts were a mile away. Her soft blond hair was again pulled into her neat bun and her unwrinkled clothing lay carefully across her body, a striking contrast to Jeremiah, whose collar was standing up on one side and who might have missed a button on his shirt somewhere along the way judging from the way

86

that his shirt bunched up strangely beneath his sweater vest. He was trying to get Kabe's attention to talk to him while Kabe casually avoided eye contact.

Everett shook his head as he moved toward the group. His group. He was disappointed that the only available seat was next to Sonniy. He was too far across the table from Greta to talk with her and was bursting to discuss the facility that he had just seen. He assumed that she had seen it on one of her tours. Their shared love of nature made him want to hear about her experiences there, and he also thought that she might know something about Landon Perry and his crew.

Without Greta to talk to, Everett ate his snack in silence and tried to create a mental bridge of the facility. He figured that it would be part of his assignment that night anyway.

Everett got to see what Kabe had been scanning the room for when the boy suddenly got out of his chair and crossed the room to the *originals'* table. A tall blond *original* that looked somewhat like Kabe had just entered the room and sat down. He looked up in surprise when Kabe tapped his shoulder and stood up awkwardly. Kabe shook the *original's* hand as the other *originals* looked on with a mixture of surprise and horror on their faces.

Kabe was speaking animatedly and gesturing with excitement. He seemed to be saying good-bye and was edging away from the table when he suddenly stepped back toward the table and gave the older boy a hug, nearly knocking him over.

Kabe smiled as he made his way back to his table. Apparently, he had not noticed the look of horror on the faces of the *originals,* nor did he note it on the faces of his friends.

"That's my cousin Jace!" he told them. "My aunt and uncle brought him here when he was ten months old. They said that they just couldn't keep up with him and thought that he would be better stimulated and better understood here. He's older than me, so I've never met him before, but I could tell who he is because he looks just like my uncle."

Kabe was obviously excited about finding his cousin, and no one felt that it would be a good time to tell him about the problem with the *originals*. A cloud darkened Jeremiah's face and he faced away from Kabe for the rest of the snack period. Everett wondered if Jace had been part of the attack that Jeremiah had suffered earlier in the day or if Jeremiah just reacted that way to any of the *originals*.

The snack break was soon over, and the group got up to walk to Mr. Elan's class. Everett noticed with curiosity that Jace looked over his shoulder briefly at Kabe's group as he headed into the hallway. His expression was a mixture of regret and concern as he looked at his young cousin, and Everett wondered if the attractive boy with an *original* for a cousin might actually escape the hazing portion of his ORIENTATION.

The group was quiet as they walked down the hallway. The most talkative of the group, Kimin, was lost in thought. When Sonniy asked her if she was all right, Kimin smiled briefly and mentioned that she was thinking about Mr. Dodd's class. Everett remembered the discussion about the EMOTIONAL OE and that they were supposed to discuss managing strategies with Mr. Elan.

A flood of emotions temporarily froze him. He was overwhelmed by the diverse feelings that he had surrounding this school, his mother, and his conceptualization about his future. Just a few days ago, he'd had no question that he would grow up safe in his mother's home. He had planned to secure an apprenticeship for a trade or work for an animal husbandry facility when he was old enough to join the WORKFORCE. His mother had always been an integral part of that picture.

Instead, he would grow up in a school that was both wonderful and frightening to him. He could now pursue courses in the MASTERY field of his choice and might one day be given the coveted G tattoo to proudly show the world. Although that prospect excited him, he did not know how his mother fit into that future.

Kabe and Sonniy separated from the group at the doorway of Mr. Elan's classroom.

"Our robots got a message from Mr. Elan that said that we can take an extended tour of the facility today. He only wants to meet with the students that connected with the EMOTIONAL OE," Sonniy explained. "We'll see you at rec time!"

Surprised, the rest of the group walked into the classroom without comment. Kimin and Jeremiah walked over to the window to gaze outside. Everett wanted to talk to Greta about his tour, but she looked pensive and distracted, so he took a seat and leaned forward with his elbows on his knees.

"Well, this is a solemn group! I think that you are the quietest that I have ever heard you!" Mr. Elan said, feigning mock surprise as he entered.

His familiarity with the group caused Everett to realize that his friends had been at the SFGP longer than him, which meant that they would each finish their ORIENTATION soon.

Would he even have these friends in a week?

He smiled wryly as he thought, *I guess I can add anxiety to my growing list of emotions.*

Mr. Elan invited the group to lie on the floor with their faces looking up at the ceiling. They shifted around until everyone was positioned comfortably, and Mr. Elan dimmed the lights. His voice became soft as he asked them to close their eyes. He told them that they might feel a slight adrenal response as they began to relinquish control and instructed them to breathe through the feeling with long, deep breaths.

Everett felt a wave of nausea in his stomach as he felt a loss of control and his muscles screamed at him to get up. He took long, deep breathes until he began to feel a deep sense of calm and switched to shallow, comfortable breaths. A kaleidoscope of colors played on his eyelids. Dark and light orange spots interplayed on a black background, and he lost himself for a time as he studied them. He was actually startled when he finally heard Mr. Elan's soft voice.

"The EMOTIONAL OVEREXCITABILITY can be a challenging and deeply personal experience. You have been given a great and unusual capacity to care. There can be a vast *depth* to the emotions that you feel, which can lead you to develop extraordinary attachments and bonds to people and animals. You have the capacity for empathy, which allows you to perceive what others are feeling, and sometimes experience those emotions along with them."

He paused and the soft sound of breathing filled the room.

"You have a great depth and range of emotions. You judge your actions and reactions. With this OE you may *overly* examine yourself and can become highly self-critical."

There was a long pause interrupted only by someone rustling as they shifted position.

"I want to take a moment to validate the feelings that you might have as you adjust to your life here. Some students, usually those without this OE, jump into this school with great fervor and find this a refreshing and needed change for them. Students who *have* the EMOTIONAL OE often struggle with grief over bonds that have been severed. You bond more deeply with others, and learning to be away from the people that you love can be difficult. It is also challenging to meet new people and to start new relationships."

The sound of a tearful sniff echoed in the quiet room.

"So let's talk about how to work through this. One important managing strategy is to *identify* your emotion. The physical reaction is often felt first. You may feel panic, or anxiety, or a deep sadness. Understand what you are feeling and give it a name. Sometimes there are several emotions interplaying within you at the same time, so try to separate them out."

He paused again.

"Take deep breaths. Let your heart rate slow down. Allow the heat to fade from your cheeks. Wait for your stomach to settle. Then *accept* your feelings. Remember that it is okay to have emotional reactions and that having them is part of who you are. Finally, you have to *deal* with your feelings. Identify the source. What are you feeling and why?"

Everett thought about his mother leaving him. He knew that he was feeling betrayed and confused, and he knew *why* he felt that way. The strategy that he was struggling with was learning to calm his physical reactions to those feelings. His stomach twisted every time that he thought of his mother.

"Another important strategy is to try to *prevent* emotional reactions whenever possible. Reflect on what types of activities or situations cause you to feel strong emotions. Avoid situations that cause a negative emotion. If that is not possible, you should learn to recognize the onset of an emotional reaction, like sweaty palms or butterflies in your stomach, so that you can control it. If these warning signs occur, escape the situation if possible, but if it cannot be avoided, try to calm yourself as you experience the emotion. Identify what feeling is affecting you and give yourself *permission* to feel that way. Breathe through the emotion and try to keep your reaction under control."

Mr. Elan stopped talking. His pause lasted so long that Everett peeked to see what was happening and saw that Mr. Elan and the other students were now breathing peacefully.

The steps all made great sense to Everett. He just was not sure that he could do it. His emotional reactions were intense and their onset seemed sudden. He was not sure that he could recognize the signs early enough to prevent a reaction.

The other students started to rustle, and Mr. Elan invited them to get up and stretch. He took no questions and discussed it no further. He did, however, give them each a slim metal rectangle that signaled an assignment.

The students filed out of the classroom silently, not their usual gaggle of giggling and playfully teasing children. They all had serious, thoughtful expressions and luckily had their robots to guide them forward to their recreational time. Greta and Everett both wandered to the Nature Center, although not together. They arrived at about the same time and blushed when their eyes met. As if a silent agreement had been made, they carefully took different paths.

Both children needed some time alone to think about what they had learned.

Everett wandered into a relatively barren area of the enclosure. Sharp jagged rocks jutted out in strange places and scrubby plants pushed forth from deep cracks. He ran his fingers along the sharp, open edges and along the face of the outcropping as its smooth but grainy texture invigorated his senses.

He thought back to what Sev had shared about Landon and his fellow students seeking to study nature away from the natural world. It was something that he couldn't quite understand because he thought that he would love the adventure and the danger of being exposed to the elements, surviving off of the land, and experiencing the dynamic and unpredictable side of nature.

While he understood the logic of creating a controlled environment for scientific study and experimentation, he also could not imagine staying in a laboratory for the rest of his life. Maybe that was why Landon had decided to become an astronaut. What could be more exciting than studying a completely unknown land? A shiver crept down his back at the thought.

As he ran his fingers along the thick, rubbery edge of a plant, he thought about the steps that Mr. Elan had given him to deal with his emotions and realized that his mother used to identify his emotions for him.

She would say, "Everett, you are reacting this way because you are feeling *frustrated*. You want to make your picture look just like the real thing, but your hands have not developed enough dexterity in them to make small strokes due to your age. When you feel frustrated, you should take deep breaths, look at your painting again, and find at least two positive things that you can say about it."

A scowl crossed his handsome face and he reached up to shove his dark hair, now sweaty from the humid enclosure, off of his forehead.

Why did so many signs point to the fact that his mother could have been a student here?

Expectations

Everett met up with his friends as they converged in the hallway. Sev motioned him away from the group, and Everett was frustrated to be separated from his friends again, especially when he realized with a sinking feeling that he had been led back to Sindra's office. He had thought that he only had to see her once a day, but it seemed like she popped up a lot more than that.

He wondered if his friends saw their advisors as often as he did.

Sindra smiled as he entered and gestured around the room. In his absence, she had been busy adding more posters and pictures to the wall.

He gave her a weak, congratulatory smile as he settled into his chair.

She took that as an affirmation that he liked her work and eagerly pointed out the people in the pictures. He got up to scan the walls with his hands clasped behind his back. As he browsed through the posters, he began to notice that all of the people had something in common. They all had the G tattoo.

He dutifully made this observation to Sindra because he knew that she was probably hoping that he would.

She nearly bounced with excitement at his observation.

"Yes, all of these people have earned the G tattoo. They are responsible for many of the advancements that humans have made in the years since this school was founded. That lady right there is the one who created the mathematical formula that allowed other scientists to understand how the ocean is pressurized, which lead other scientists and engineers to create the technology needed to build the Intercontinental Oceanic Tunnel Transit System," she said as she pointed up to the poster of a wizened, elderly woman with dark skin and gray hair.

Sindra gestured to another poster that had the letters ICOTTS spelled out in large letters over a picture of a train moving under a glass dome with sharks and fish swimming above it. Everett had heard of the train system that had been built under the ocean. It connected all of the world's continents and made intercontinental travel fast, efficient, and safe.

Seeing that Everett was impressed, she sat back, triumphant at last.

"So, how has it been going?" she asked.

Everett became guarded again as he thought about his morning; seeing Jeremiah huddled in the hallway, learning about his EMOTIONAL OE, the strange competitive feeling that he felt when he was with Kabe, the distance that he was feeling with Greta, the excitement that he had felt in the Natural Sciences wing, and the unsettling draw that he felt toward Landon Perry.

A sinking feeling overcame him as he wondered if the strategies that he had learned in Mr. Elan's class would be enough to manage the emotions that caused his stomach to churn or keep out the thoughts about his abandonment that came unbidden into his mind.

Would identifying those feelings and breathing deeply really cure that?

As he felt his stomach tighten, he tried to sort out the emotions that he was feeling. Frustration filtered through him as he remembered Jeremiah pleading with him not to tell anyone that the *originals* had bullied him. Then he thought about Greta not speaking to him. His stomach still twisted as he struggled to understand the dynamics of his friendship with her. Rationally, he knew that she had already forgiven him, but he still worried that her opinion of him had changed.

He sighed audibly at this thought and then flushed when he realized that he had never answered Sindra's question. He had been lost in thought while she had waited patiently, which told him that she must be a good listener.

"Well, I have a lot of emotions that I am trying to sort out right now," he finally told her.

She nodded, and a comfortable silence stretched between them. As she waited, he tried to sort through which emotion he wanted her help with. Any emotion that was tied to his mother was still too strong and too painful to talk about with Sindra yet, if ever. He wanted to share his anger and frustration with her about the *originals,* but he had broached that subject before and had faced a blank wall. That left him with his new emotions about having friends and being unsure of what the expectations were in a group.

"You know more about me than anyone at this school does," he said finally. "You and other Observers have watched me "play" with the other children in my classes throughout the years. My mother had to train me to do that. She wanted me to stay near the other children

94

and to act interested in what they were doing and saying. That was really hard for me. It's not that I thought that I was better than the other kids or anything. I just couldn't relate to them. Now that I am here, I do like a few of the other children. There is one student that I have really connected to. She-she is interested in nature and in science and she-well, she just feels *comfortable* to me. Does that make sense?"

Sindra nodded.

"It absolutely makes sense to me Everett. I have had a few friends like that in my life, but not many. You are lucky to have found such a friend. So what concerns you about this situation?" she asked kindly.

Everett ran his fingers along the stitching on the chair cushion.

"Well, yesterday I didn't even have to work at making friends," he continued. "A few of the girls in my class just let me into their group. They ate with me, and showed me around the rec center, and they even sent me a message at night to say that they were glad to have met me. Then today, I saw something that upset me before class, and I ignored them because I just didn't want to talk at the moment. They both were a little mad and ignored me for a while. Now they are talking to me again, but there is this new boy in our class, and they seem to like him just as much as they like me, and now I don't know if we will even get to *stay* friends because their ORIENTATION will end before mine and I don't know if we will even have classes together." His words came out in a disorganized flood, which bothered him because he preferred to speak with precision.

Sindra nodded understandingly, and he could tell that she had understood him.

"So let's sort out these emotions," she said. "You have made *connections* with new people. You are feeling insecure about your new friendships. You are feeling that your grasp on your friends is tenuous."

Everett nodded his head, actually impressed at how precisely Sindra had identified his feelings.

She continued with a slight smile, "As you get to know them, you will be tuned into your friends' reactions to what you do and say, possibly looking for evidence of judgments being made, and hoping for signs of acceptance. This is natural Everett. It is new for you to connect with children in your age bracket. In the past, you *observed*

95

other children at play and probably watched as alliances formed and broke and reformed. Although you are aware of how children interact, you are new to truly experiencing it. I would say that you are excited, hopeful, nervous, and fearful of losing the friendships that have just started to form. Do you have any changes or additions to that list of emotions?"

Everett shook his head.

"Now that we know what to call the emotions, what are you having the hardest time dealing with?" she asked softly.

"Kimin is so fun and interesting, and she lifts my spirits. So the negative side to that is that I wonder what I will feel like if I lose her friendship. Greta is so calming and intriguing. She and I have so many things in common that I feel like I can totally be myself with her. I feel like I don't have to pretend to like everything that she likes, mostly because I really do, but also because I feel like it wouldn't bother her if I disagreed with her. I've never really had a friend, though, so I guess I just feel scared that I might do something wrong and lose her as a friend," he admitted.

"The fear of loss, whether in the near future or in the distant future, *can* be very worrisome Everett, and unfortunately I cannot tell you that you *will* stop worrying about it. That is the advice that often comes from people *without* this OVEREXCITABILITY. They will tell you to just "stop worrying" as if it was a choice," she said with an eye roll.

"What I *can* tell you," she continued, "is to accept those feelings and acknowledge that having those anxieties is a part of who you are. They are not wrong, but they *can* be prioritized and set aside so that you can focus on other things. I think of *my* anxieties as a packet, which I wrap up and set aside when I have other things to deal with. But I also picture that they are stored in an overly stuffed closet and that sometimes I open the door to that closet and the worries fall out when I am least expecting them. Then I either have to deal with them or put them back."

Her analogy made sense to Everett. It was like his worry about being found by an Observer. Most of the time, the worry had been in the back of his mind, like Sindra's closet. But sometimes, when he least expected it, a feeling of dread would wash down his entire body, and he would think, *I hope that no one saw me do that,* or *what if a letter will come today that will send me away?*

Like Sindra had said, in the past he had been able to get that feeling under control and push it away, like putting it back in the closet.

"I like your analogy," he said shyly.

"I'm glad!" she said with a smile. "We will continue to discuss this, Everett, but unfortunately our time has ended. I know that you have a multitude of emotions that you are processing right now. My advice to you is to embrace the friendships that you have made, and allow your friends to help you work through some of this. If you are unsure about what their expectations of you are, it can help for you to ask them directly. That way, you never have to wonder."

Everett nodded as he stood up. He had to admit that it was actually good advice. Instead of worrying about what *might* make them stop being his friend, he could just ask them. That way he would know what *not* to do.

He flashed Sindra a brief but genuine smile as he left her office. She smiled softly at the hurting young boy who was so bravely embracing his new situation and looked at the posters that filled her office walls. She had the feeling that he too would do something special one day, and she was proud the she had discovered him.

Everett followed Sev back to the refreshment area for a mid-day meal. Yesterday, he had been too overwhelmed by this point in the day to continue and had taken a break in his dormitory. Today, he could not wait to see his friends again and to figure out what it would take to keep their friendships.

As he scanned the faces across the room to find his friends, he accidentally bumped into the boy ahead of him. The boy turned around, glowering, and looked ready to fight. Everett swallowed the apology that had automatically sprung to his lips when he saw that the other boy was Jace, Kabe's cousin, and an *original*.

He remembered Jeremiah's reaction to Kabe talking to Jace that morning, and any fear that he might have otherwise felt as he faced the tall, powerful boy faded. Contempt took the place of his fear, and he felt it filling his veins.

"Excuse me," he ground out to Jace, who was now deliberately blocking his path. Jace's arms were crossed and a sneer marred his handsome face. When he realized that the *transplant* sounded defiant rather than frightened, he took a small step back in surprise and momentarily lowered his crossed arms.

Everett took advantage of the other boy's indecision and stepped around him. By the time Jace recovered, he would have had to follow behind Everett and grab his arm to confront him, which would be too overt for an *original* in such a crowded place.

Everett had the feeling that there would be retribution later and shivered with fear.

He grabbed his meal and quickly found his friends at a table on the far wall. Grateful to see a space open next to Greta, he slid in next to her with a sheepish smile on his face. She returned his smile and then looked quizzically across the room at Jace, who was still staring in Everett's direction.

"What happened?" she whispered, aware that Kabe was sitting only a few seats away.

"I accidently stepped on his heel, and he turned around, all puffed up and menacing. When he wouldn't get out of my way, I stepped around him. I think that he wanted to follow me, but in this crowd he has to be more discreet. Hopefully I'll be around tomorrow," he joked.

Greta's face went from surprised, to impressed, to worried.

"Remember Everett, we only have to face them for one week. After that, they will leave you alone, *if* you don't make an issue of it!" she warned.

He was about to snap at Greta, but stopped himself when he realized that she was only concerned for him. His anger smoldered deep inside of him, but he took Sindra's advice and tucked the feeling away to deal with later.

"I went to the Natural Sciences wing today," he told Greta, hoping to change to a more comfortable subject.

Her face lit up, and she pounced on him with questions and comments about the facility.

The meal flew by as Everett and Greta ate quick bites between words. They both wanted the other's opinions on what they had seen and shared their ideas about what else the facility must hold.

It lifted Everett's spirits to know that another child his age shared his passionate interest in nature and science.

Kimin made a half-joking comment about how they had left everyone else out of their conversation as the group got up to leave.

98

Greta flushed, and Everett was about to defend their actions when he remembered Sindra's advice. *If you are unsure about what their expectations of you are, it can help for you to ask them directly. That way, you never have to wonder.*

He realized that instead of feeling defensive, he should take Kimin's comment as her expectation for group discussions.

"I'm sorry if you thought that we were rude for leaving you out," he said sincerely.

Kimin looked surprised, as if she had not expected him to acknowledge her comment.

"Thanks Everett. I just think that everyone at the table should be included in the conversation," she replied.

He thought back to the other meals that they had shared as a group. Although Kimin did tend to dominate the conversations, she *was* always trying to bring others into the conversation and asked for opinions and comments from everyone. He nodded to accept her preference and figured that he could use his rec time to talk to Greta privately.

Surprisingly, Sonniy spoke up to disagree with Kimin and said, "I think that we can all respect the fact that we won't always want to talk about the same things. Greta and Everett shouldn't have to wait until a different time to talk to each other just because they want to talk about something that only interests them. You *do* include everyone in the conversation, Kimin, but you also usually pick the topic. I don't think that we should have to search for a topic that *all* six people can talk about for every single meal."

The group was briefly shocked into silence. It was strange to hear Sonniy disagree with Kimin because she always seemed to do whatever Kimin was doing.

Everett scanned the faces of his friends. Kimin's body language told him that she was upset and defensive about Sonniy's comment. Jeremiah looked nervous and kept looking back and forth between Kimin and Sonniy. Greta was still flushed and looked queasy. Kabe looked irritated, although Everett was not sure about what.

"Why don't we all think about this problem and talk about it during our rec time?" Kabe finally suggested.

Everyone nodded slowly in agreement, and the tense group moved into the hallway.

Kabe's words surprised Everett. For some reason, he had not considered Kabe a part of the group. He had judged Kabe rather quickly that morning. Kabe's good looks and confidence had made Everett fit him into a category of people that were self-concerned and arrogant. He was ashamed to realize that he had put Kabe into that category based on a stereotype and not because he had actually shown any of those qualities.

Kabe seemed to think of himself as part of this little band of children and was invested in its future. Everett decided to make more of an effort with the other boy.

The disjointed group filed silently into Mr. Dodd's classroom. He was already there, which meant that they were late. He had a broad smile on his face, until he read the mood of the group. The children had seated themselves somewhat far apart from each other, and they all had tense or uncomfortable expressions.

Mr. Dodd cleared his throat and asked, "Do you all need to discuss something?"

His voice was kind, but his tone was firm. It said that they could discuss their problem if they wanted to, but that they could not sulk the entire class period.

They exchanged glances and then looked away.

"We agreed to take some time to think about our problem before we discuss it again," Kabe said politely to Mr. Dodd.

Mr. Dodd nodded as he looked around the room at the children's faces and then grabbed a handful of bags. As he handed them out, some of the student eagerly delved into their bags, while others waited politely for instructions.

Everett peeked into his bag and saw a variety of shapes of different colors and sizes. He glanced over at Greta and was not surprised to see that she had not opened her bag. All eyes turned expectantly to Mr. Dodd, who smothered a smile and turned his back on the class to look out the window with his hands in his pockets.

The children looked around at each other in confusion. Kabe finally shrugged and dumped his bag out onto the floor. Greta and Everett both turned to look at Mr. Dodd, not sure how the instructor would react to Kabe emptying his bag without permission.

Mr. Dodd kept his back turned, and one by one, the students spread out with their bags and opened them up. Greta was the last student to open her bag.

Everett went to the back corner of the room, sat down, and dumped out his bag. A variety of options jumped out at him. He loved to categorize things, and these items could be organized by size, shape, and color.

His fingers roved over the items as he itched to begin sorting them. As he began to collect the red shapes, he suddenly hesitated. What if sorting them by characteristics was too simple? Was this a trick?

Feeling a sense of panic, he looked around the room. The other students were shielding their piles from everyone else, and Mr. Dodd had moved to sit at his desk by the door. He had no one to tell him what to do and no one to judge his choices. It was an exciting but frightening feeling.

Free to just think about what *he* wanted to do, he looked at the shapes again. Several ideas bounced through his mind before he realized that he could sort them using more than one characteristic.

He placed the shapes into the rough outline of a circle and made sections of red, orange, blue, and green items. Within the sections of color, he further separated the items by shape. He ended up with a red stripe of triangles, a red stripe of circles, and a red stripe of squares, which completed the red section of the overall circle.

Although he was still bothered that he had not sorted them by size, he completed the same pattern for all of the shapes and then rocked back on his heels to look it over. Suddenly, he realized that he could put the largest shapes at the perimeter of the circle and complete each row in descending order of size.

He felt immensely satisfied and looked up to find that Mr. Dodd was looking at his circle with an appreciative smile that went all the way to his eyes.

Mr. Dodd invited the students to walk around and look at what the other students had created. Feeling eager to see what the others had done, but insecure about them looking at his creation, Everett headed over to see what Greta had made. He found it interesting that she had also categorized the items by size, color, and shape, but she had arranged her shapes into separate rectangles of color.

Moving on, he saw that Kabe and Kimin had used the shapes to create three-dimensional sculptures that were interesting to look at from all different sides. Panic froze him for a moment as he wondered if *they* had done it the right way and he and Greta had been wrong.

Sonniy had stacked the shapes in towers of the same shape in descending order of size. It did not seem like she had used color to organize them at all.

Everett looked around for Jeremiah's creation and saw with concern that his shapes were in the same pile that he had started with when he had dumped them out. Looking for Jeremiah, he saw the tall boy in the corner with his back to the class. His body was hunched forward, and Mr. Dodd was trying to calm him down.

Kimin moved over to Everett and whispered, "He's upset because he doesn't want to do the activity the wrong way. Mr. Dodd told him that there *is* no wrong way, but Jeremiah doesn't believe him."

Everett nodded because he had felt the same way. Their EDUCATIONAL EXPERIENCES must have been similar.

Finally, Mr. Dodd coaxed Jeremiah to look at the other children's creations.

"You see, everyone approached this activity a little differently. Some students grouped the items by characteristics that were similar, and others used them as an art medium to create a sculpture," he told Jeremiah as he swept his hand around the classroom.

Jeremiah nodded tearfully and wiped his eyes before smiling at his instructor and his classmates.

Sonniy raised her hand and asked, "So who did it the right way? Who won?"

Mr. Dodd shook his head sadly and motioned for everyone to join him on the floor.

"There is not a right *or* wrong way to approach this activity. The way that you approached this activity can tell you a little about your CREATIVE THINKING ABILITY. If you have a STRENGTH in this area, you are *full* of ideas. Not only will you think of ideas that no one else has thought of before, you will also be able to take the ideas or inventions of others and see multiple ways for them to be changed or improved. You might think of possibilities that others see as strange or impossible. One idea may initiate a multitude of other ideas. How many of you made the very first thing that you thought of?" he asked.

Sonniy raised her hand with a shrug.

"How many of you thought of several options, and then once you thought of an idea, elaborated on it several times before you got to your final product?" he asked, raising his eyebrows.

Everett thought about how he had started with two characteristics, but was not satisfied until he had found a way to make all three characteristics work, and raised his hand.

"If you have this ability and are given a problem to work on that has no obvious solution, you will think of many different ways to approach it," Mr. Dodd continued. "It won't bother you that there is no clear solution, because the challenge will stimulate you. You might think of solutions that are not obvious to other people, because you can connect ideas in unusual ways. You will have the persistence to try to solve the problem, again and again, no matter how many times you fail. You will not have this same attention for *all* of the activities that you do. The project has to interest you, but once it does, you can become tireless in your quest to reach a solution."

After dismissing the class, Mr. Dodd held Jeremiah back as the other students filed out of the classroom for recreational time. Ordinarily, Everett looked forward to rec time, but his stomach dropped as he entered the rec center because he knew that he and his friends were going to discuss the problem that had arisen during the mid-day meal.

Jeremiah caught up to the group, and with a few glances at each other and some non-verbal gestures, they found a corner to settle into. They sat in a rough semi-circle and looked around at each other, not sure who should start talking first. Everett looked at Kimin because she was usually the first one to speak and saw that her face was somewhat red and puffy.

Suddenly, she burst out with angry tears, "I am sorry if you all think that I'm trying to control everything that you do!"

Greta looked shocked and placed a gentle hand on Kimin's arm. She quietly reassured her that no one had said that. Kimin looked away but seemed to calm a little at Greta's words.

Kabe said, "Look, I've always had a hard time fitting in with the other kids in my EDUCATIONAL EXPERIENCES, but whenever I had a problem with my siblings and my cousins, we just gave everyone the chance to share their feelings and then we looked for common ground. I don't think that anyone has been blamed for anything. We just have to figure out what we all need from this friendship."

Everett was surprised that Kabe had made such articulate points and decided to speak up next.

"I'm also struggling to understand how to interact with a large group of kids," he said. "I appreciate you all for pulling me into your group and accepting me so easily. Even though I enjoy group conversations, sometimes I just want to talk to one person, and sometimes I don't even want to talk at all. This morning I didn't talk to Kimin and Greta because I was upset about something else, and I felt like both of you were mad at me for it. I also tried to speak to Greta privately at the mid-day meal, because I knew that she was interested in what I would be saying, but I wasn't sure if anyone else would be. Both times, someone was upset with me. I want to be able to make choices without feeling like I'm risking that someone will get mad at me."

Sonniy nodded vigorously in agreement.

Kimin's face clouded into a defensive frown when she realized that she had been part of both incidences. Greta's face showed that she agreed with Everett, but she stayed silent and kept her supportive hand on Kimin's arm. Jeremiah looked like he was about to cry.

Finally, Kimin said, "Well, I didn't have an easy time making friends during my EDUCATIONAL EXPERIENCES either. I found that no one wanted to hear what I wanted to talk about but that I would be included if I talked about things that everyone else liked. I turned into a chatterbox because it felt good to have people to talk to, even if I was not interested in what we were talking about. I felt left out when they would turn to each other to talk about something that I couldn't relate to. So I guess I just feel more secure when everyone is talking together, because that is how I felt accepted before."

The group was silent for a long moment while they each considered Kimin's words. Everett had never felt the need to feel accepted by his peers, probably because his mother had set the expectation that he would not be, but he could relate to what Kimin was saying. In his first experience with being in a group yesterday, he had felt comforted by the ongoing chatter and by Kimin's efforts to involve him in the conversation.

After the long pause, Greta said, "It sounds to me like the message that we all have in common, which is what Kabe said to look for, is that we are all happy to have each other as friends. That means that we really don't have to worry anymore about being accepted, because we all *have* accepted each other. That should make us feel like we can interact with each other as a group, as pairs, and even not at all. I think that we should just agree that if we have a problem with each other, we will be open and honest about it. That way, we can assume that if someone walks away, they just need some time alone."

Sonniy, Kabe, and Everett nodded and smiled at her words. Kimin took a few moments longer than the rest, but a slow smile finally cracked the angry scowl that had been on her face, and she nodded her agreement. Jeremiah looked relieved that the tension had eased, and Everett realized that he had never asked Greta what Jeremiah had shared with the group when Everett had gone to the Nature Center alone.

Thinking of that, he looked longingly toward the blissful escape into the world of plants and animals. Greta followed his gaze and was about to speak when they both noticed that the group's robots were traveling toward them in a long band. Everett sighed and thought that they were not given enough time in this facility. He wondered if that might change when his ORIENTATION was over, but somehow he did not think so.

He waved a sorrowful good-bye to his friends and followed Sev back to his dormitory.

Connections

Everett desperately wanted a shower when he got back to his room and had already opened the shower stall door when Sev protested that he should eat first. He ignored the robot and cranked the water to the hottest setting. As he enjoyed the sensation of hot water on his skin, he wondered if enjoying hot showers was part of his SENSUAL OVEREXCITABILITY.

Sev seemed to be sulking when he padded back into the room in his loose, silky nightclothes. The robot had already ordered Everett's meal for him, and he was irritated to find that it was the same meal that he had eaten the night before. Everett enjoyed variety in his meals, but one look at Sev told Everett that if he expressed any dissatisfaction, the robot would only point out that he should have ordered the meal himself before taking a shower.

He shook his head as he sat down at the table and wolfed down the food, glad that he had taken the time to shower and get comfortable anyway.

As soon as Everett had swallowed the last bite, Sev whisked away the tray and placed his silver tablet and stylus in front of him.

"You must complete last night's assignment before you can start on the assignment that you received today," the robot informed him.

Everett groaned. He felt like protesting, but realized that unlike at home, where he would fill the evening hours reading with his mother, helping her cook, playing games of strategy, or just sharing his thoughts with her, the only choice that he had here besides doing his work was sleeping.

He was not tired yet, so he turned on the SKEtch pad and pulled up the bridge that he had started the day before. Under *friends* he added the names Sonniy, Jeremiah, and hesitantly, Kabe. He went back to the cogwheel, highlighted *tour*, and then tapped the looking glass. He saw the word that he had written the day before, only his emotion, *confused,* and shook his head as he realized that today's tour had left him with an entirely different set of feelings.

Without hesitation, he eagerly sketched the most exciting parts of the Life and Natural Sciences Wing. He sketched the deep sea simulator, the towering trees and diverse organisms of the rain forest, and the equipment that he had noticed in the laboratories. His stylus flew across the screen as his brain overflowed with images, fragments of thoughts, ideas, and questions.

As he added a final detail to his sketch of the rain forest, he recalled the story of the five students that had put so much effort into promoting the creation of the facility. He remembered the photograph of Landon Perry and the look of pride in his eyes. He also thought of the poster in Sindra's office that showed Landon as part of the first crew to set foot on Mars.

What an interesting person, Everett thought.

Everett moved back to the main wheel, highlighted the topic *advisor,* and zoomed to it with the looking glass tool. His emotion word from the day before was *irritated.* He flushed momentarily and felt bad that he had used that word for Sindra, because his impression of her today was much improved. After some consideration, he left it there, realizing that at some point he might want to look back through his journey at this school. He added the words *trying, interested,* and *cowardly.*

Sindra *was* trying to get to know him better and to engage him in conversation, which pleased him even though he knew that it was her job to get more information about him. At times, he felt that she really *was* interested in him, and it made him feel a little special to think of all of the time that she had put into discovering him. Her refusal to address his remark about the *originals* made him think of her as a coward, and because of that, she did not yet have Everett's respect. He also did not feel as though he could trust her yet.

He went back to the main wheel to look at his other topics and selected *originals,* because he could not judge Sindra for avoiding the topic if he did not face it himself. Yesterday's words had been *anger* and *frustration.* He added the names Dre and Jace and then wrote about finding Jeremiah huddled in a corner crying. He frowned as he recalled the incident and wished that he knew more about what had happened.

He was about to go back to the main wheel when he remembered Kabe's connection to Jace. He wrote Kabe next to Jace and then drew a line to connect them. Finally, he added a pair of binoculars by Jace to remind himself to watch out for the *original.* Their brief interaction that afternoon had left Everett with no doubt that he would eventually have some kind of altercation with the larger boy.

Everett zoomed back to the main wheel and saw that he needed to add information to *classes* and *new understandings*.

He selected *classes* first and jotted down DABROWSKI, GENERAL INTELLECTUAL ABILITY, OVEREXCITABILITIES, SPECIFIC ACADEMIC APTITUDE, MANAGING STRATEGIES, TOOLS, and CREATIVE THINKING ABILITY. It was not the exact order in which he had learned about the topics, but he wrote them in the order that he thought of them.

Carefully, he put the SKEtch pad down on his table and got up to walk to have some time to think. As he walked around the perimeter of his bed, he remembered that it was possible to record his voice while using the SKEtch pad.

Sev had already entered his sleep mode, but the robot had told him that he could activate him, and Everett was excited to learn how to use this new function. Besides, he was still a trifle irritated with Sev's meal selection.

The robot, to his credit, did not appear bothered by the interruption in the least. If anything, he seemed excited to comply with the boy's request and quickly showed him the symbol on the menu that looked like an open mouth with sound waves radiating from it. He instructed Everett to highlight the *new understandings* section and then told Everett to tap the recording icon. A blue light came on and Everett hesitantly spoke.

"This is Everett."

When Sev sensed that the boy was finished, he showed him where to tap to stop recording. The SKEtch pad was heat activated and had previously only worked when Everett was holding it. Sev showed him the button that would keep the machine activated without the touch of his hands so that he could rest the pad on the table and walk around as he spoke. This new function excited Everett because he felt a nervous energy flooding him that he needed to walk off.

He shyly asked Sev to fully shut down, because he did not want to feel in any way that the robot was listening. The robot agreed and showed Everett how to turn him on again with the press of a button located under a concealed panel.

Everett took a few laps around his bed to burn off his nervous energy and waited until Sev shut down before he activated the recording feature. There was a long pause before he began, and he spoke haltingly at first. Eventually, he became fully engaged in what he was saying and forgot that he was even doing an assignment.

"I'm pretty sure that I have the SENSUAL OVEREXCITABILITY. My brain takes in so much information from my senses that it can be frustrating. I am supposed to take deep breaths and work my way through the frustration that can build when I am irritated by sounds but am powerless to make them stop. I can also set up a plan to desensitize myself to irritating sounds, which I plan to do once I get settled here. The positive thing is that I also really enjoy some of the sounds that I hear. I never saw the connection between those experiences before now."

Everett stretched his arms over his head to release tension.

"I also react to sensations that I feel when I *touch* different objects. I like to run my hands along a variety of textures, like smooth, rough, silky, and coarse. Other sensations irritate me, like hair on my forehead, which I guess goes along with the idea of having a range of reactions."

Everett chuckled when he realized that he had been toying with the seamed edge of his nightshirt and running his hand along the tabletop each time that he passed it as he talked about the SENSUAL OE.

"So that leaves me with the EMOTIONAL OVEREXCITABILITY. This one is hard for me to talk about, even to myself. I've never had a close friend, until maybe Greta, but I've never talked with other kids about how they feel about their mothers. I know that I feel an intense love for my mother. Mr. Dodd talked about making strong bonds with some people and feeling intense emotions. The bond that I share with my mother has always felt like a link, like a life force that we share. That probably sounds weird when I say it out loud, but maybe you shouldn't try to put that feeling into words."

A pain radiated through his torso as he realized how much he *missed* his mother.

"Mr. Dodd talked about an emotional memory that makes feelings stay with people for a long time. I feel a gut-wrenching sensation anytime that I am nervous, and I remember the details of each and every time that I've been embarrassed. Mr. Elan went over some managing strategies with us, but to be honest, I don't think that they will work. I find it hard to believe that I just have to breathe deeply and all of my anger and hurt over my mother leaving me will just disappear."

His heart started thumping as the feelings of betrayal resurfaced, and he took several deep, ragged breaths. His heart rate did drop somewhat, but the deep, bitter pain remained and buried itself into the pit of his stomach.

"I also connected with the CREATIVE THINKING ABILITY. I am always thinking about ways to improve things, both by changing things that already exist and by creating new inventions. My mom always wrote my ideas down in a journal for me, even after I was able to write on my own. She liked to hear my ideas..."

He stopped recording. He wanted to move on to the next assignment and hoped that it had nothing to do with the EMOTIONAL OVEREXCITABILITY.

He pushed the button to wake Sev up and realized that it would take longer for Sev to wake up from his powered off setting than from his sleep mode. While he waited, he sipped on his beverage and forced his mind to settle, pushing away thoughts of his mother every time that they crept in. He pictured the packet that Sindra had referred to and imagined wrapping up his feelings about his mother and pushing them into a dark closet.

Relief washed over him when Sev's voice finally pulled him away from his thoughts. "Good evening Everett. I will now show you the video message for tonight's assignment," the robot announced.

Everett groaned when he saw Mr. Elan on the screen because he figured that it meant that there would be an assignment about the EMOTIONAL OE. A wave of nausea washed over him as he waited to hear his assignment.

"You have discovered that you experience the EMOTIONAL OVEREXCITABILITY. You will have many new and challenging emotions to deal with as you adjust to your life at this school. You are feeling loss, you are struggling to form friendships, and you may feel confused. It may take you a long time to sort through these emotions. Rather than have you work through feelings that you are not ready to address yet, I am going to show you some of the positive aspects of the SENSUAL OVEREXCITABILITY. This OE allows you to experience sensations on a deep and meaningful level. If any of the sensory input that you experience during this activity makes you uncomfortable, please touch your screen to move on to the next example. Robot Number Seventeen, please assist Everett with the materials needed for this activity."

Mr. Elan was gone with a wink and a smile, and a menu of media popped up. Sev pulled a variety of objects and bottles out of his pouch and laid them out on the table. He explained to Everett that his assignment was to experience a variety of sensory experiences, such as hearing music, viewing images of artwork or scenes from nature, and touching and smelling the items on the table. He was supposed to use his extensive vocabulary to identify the emotion brought forward by each experience.

Everett started with a video of the most breathtaking sunset that he had ever seen and quickly lost himself in the beauty of each sensory experience. After a full hour of experiences, he was filled with a profound sense of joy and wonder.

He crawled into bed that night feeling deeply satisfied and utterly exhausted.

Identity

Sindra was about to leave when a call alerted her that the Chancellor needed to see her. She held back a sigh of irritation. The Chancellor was not her direct supervisor, but she had to be respectful of him because her work was so closely connected with the school.

She reflected on Everett's progress as she walked to his office. Everett's first day had been difficult, but his attitude had changed dramatically once he had made a few friends. She had also noted the excitement in his voice that morning when she had asked him about his classes. It seemed that he was interested in his gifted CHARACTERISTICS and was beginning to view himself in a new and more understanding way. He had even given her a friendly smile when he left her office that afternoon.

She wondered why the Chancellor would need to see her so urgently at the end of the day when her only mentee seemed to be adjusting much better than expected. The door silently slid open as she waved her badge over the access panel at the end of his hallway. She took the remaining steps down the hallway to his office and was surprised to find that the door was open.

The Chancellor was sitting with his chair faced to look out of the window. She felt a pang of discomfort when she saw the pensive look on his face as he glanced over his shoulder at her and motioned her into the office. Normally the Chancellor would meet her at his office door, shake her hand, and invite her in with a broad smile.

A much different man sat before her now.

Sindra slid into the chair opposite his desk and waited for him to speak. After a few moments, he swiveled his chair to face her and gave her a brief smile.

"Sindra, I am about to tell you something that is very important, but it is also something that I would like to keep completely between us," he said slowly and carefully, keeping his eyes locked on her the entire time.

Sindra shifted uncomfortably in her chair as she nodded her acceptance of his terms.

He sat back in relief, placed his fingers in a triangle in front of his mouth and tapped his mouth a few times as he composed his thinking.

"You found a very interesting candidate for our school Sindra," he said finally. "He is unprecedented in many ways. First, he was difficult to identify as a POTENTIAL because he so carefully hid his abilities from his teachers and from Observers. As far as we can tell, he feared being identified as a POTENTIAL. Second, he deliberately sabotaged the tests that he took at our school, and we have never accepted a student that was unable to willingly demonstrate their abilities on the tests before. Finally, Everett is the only student that I have ever accepted *without* parental permission."

He watched Sindra's face carefully for her reaction and saw a mixture of shock and confusion.

"I don't understand," she replied finally.

"I told Everett that he had to stay at our school because his mother had signed away her rights to him. That was not true," he admitted. "Our records show that his mother was on the POD with Everett that brought him here and that she checked him in at the front desk for testing. However, we do not know where she went from that point forward. She was given a visitor's badge to use to acquire beverages and food items, but our records indicate that the card was never used. It appears that she was on a facility tour with Number Seventeen and that she slipped away from him. None of our security cameras were able to locate her, and I was unable to get a clear look at her face on the video when she was at the front desk. It seems as though she is familiar with this facility and its security features. It also seems that she did not want to be recognized. Any thoughts?"

Sindra thought back to what had always bothered her about Everett. It had always seemed strange that he so carefully concealed his intelligence, that he seemed afraid of her G tattoo, and that he seemed angry to have been identified as a POTENTIAL. He had also been unwilling to reveal anything about his mother when she had interviewed him on the first day. This was all atypical behavior, and she expressed her thoughts to the Chancellor as such. He was very interested and jotted down notes as she spoke.

"I would like to thank you, Sindra, both for your information *and* for your discretion." He allowed the last word to hang carefully in the room between them. She understood his meaning perfectly.

"Of course. This information will remain between us, in the best interest of Everett," she replied.

The Chancellor smiled widely as he stood up and shook her hand. He escorted her to the door and asked that she see herself out. Once she left, he sank back into his chair, feeling perturbed.

114

He recalled what he had said to Sindra about the mother being familiar with the facility and combined that with the information that the boy seemed to have been raised to be wary of G.

Could the boy's mother have been a former student here?

Could she be a G herself?

Based on the boy's age, she could have been at the school around the time that he had attended, although in a much younger class. Back then, students had been permitted to live at the facility or commute from home.

The Chancellor had been the one to change the rules to only allow students that lived on campus to attend. It had been his first act in his new position of power at the school.

He decided to go home and rest, but planned to spend as much time in the next few days as possible researching possible identities for Everett's mother.

A gauntlet had been dropped, and he planned to face the challenge.

Jeremiah's Story

Everett awoke the next morning and automatically ordered his morning meal before he got dressed. He put on his SFGP uniform with a sense of excitement. He was proud of the assignments that he had completed the night before and was hopeful that the easy camaraderie that he had felt with his friends would return today. He finished eating well before Sev's itinerary said that they needed to leave, which pleased the robot. Sev announced that they would start with a facility tour and could leave as early as they wanted to.

Everett was confused.

"I thought that I started every day with a visit with Sindra," he told the robot.

"That has been your schedule the last two days. Please understand that your ORIENTATION phase at this school has a flexible schedule that has been tailored to your specific needs, as your classes will be later on. Today you will tour the Human and Animal Sciences Wing. Are you ready to depart?" the robot asked.

Everett nodded excitedly. He was not sure what Human and Animal Sciences were, but he enjoyed any chance to interact with animals, so he quickly deposited his tray and followed Sev to the door.

Sev disseminated facts about the wing to Everett as they crossed a short sky bridge. Everett knew that he should pay attention to what Sev was saying as they crossed the bridge, but the rushing water that flowed beneath it fascinated him. It was not until they had crossed the bridge that Everett could tune back in to Sev's presentation.

He gathered that the Human and Animal Sciences Wing was more of a complex than a wing. It was where MASTERY students that were interested in medical research studied. They could specialize in learning to provide medical care for humans or animals. Another option was to study human and animal bodies and develop medicines, vaccines, and diets that would keep any species healthy.

There were also opportunities for behavioral research, sleep research, and even the new and exciting field of research in interplanetary space travel for humans.

Sev took Everett through the hallways and pointed out the functions of the different equipment, laboratories, and classrooms. Scientists waved him in to observe and ask questions in a few of the

117

laboratories. He observed one scientist looking at a screen that showed a tube-like shape that had colors radiating through it.

"I am researching the human appendix," the scientist explained. "Scientists have wondered about its function and purpose for many years. It has to be surgically removed from many people because it ruptures and poisons the body. I have thought for years that this organ could be turned into a weapon in the body to fight any number of diseases that plague humanity. I have made some significant progress in the past few years, especially once I found a MASTERY student that was interested in my research. Does this type of science interest you?"

The scientist's use of his intellect to solve problems for humanity moved Everett. He bowed his head in respect as he said, "I hope that I will have the honor of using my STRENGTHS in some way that will help others when I become a MASTERY student."

The man looked startled but pleased by Everett's words and smiled at him as he left.

Everett left with his mind buzzing with questions, ideas, and more emotions than he could name. He had not even realized that this area of science existed and now felt that he had two viable possibilities for his future MASTERY studies.

As he entered Mr. Dodd's room, he looked around at his friends and was relieved to see that Kimin's unclouded grin had returned, as had Greta's shy smile.

Everett felt a deep sense of relief.

Mr. Dodd swept in and encouraged the students to get out of their seats. As the confused students got out of their chairs, he swept them all aside. Kimin and Sonniy clapped their hands excitedly, and Kabe stretched with relief and rocked back and forth on his heels. Jeremiah shifted his weight from one foot to the other, for once not looking slouched and awkward. Greta and Everett fidgeted, unsure of themselves and uncomfortable with this turn of events.

Mr. Dodd expelled a hearty laugh.

"We will be talking about the PSYCHOMOTOR OE today," he said. "The PSYCHOMOTOR OVEREXCITABILITY is expressed through *movement* and *activity*. You might have been scolded in the past for your constant need to move. Your constant activity can be exhausting to those around you, but for you, it is exhausting to be still! The expressions of this OVEREXCITABILITY, like the SENSUAL OE, are also found in the general population, and these traits alone would not define someone as gifted, but *combined* with a gifted intellect and other OVEREXCITABILITIES, it can lead some gifted people to become tireless learners."

Mr. Dodd paused to let that sink in. Everett continued to admire Mr. Dodd's wonderful way of describing the OEs in a positive way, showing his students how to view these potential obstacles as powers that they could harness to achieve greatness.

"I think that removing the chairs has helped me to identify which of you have this OE. Do any of you have connections to share?" he asked.

Kabe, Kimin, Sonniy, and Jeremiah raised their hands. Kimin and Sonniy were obvious once Everett heard about the traits. Their rapid speech and constant gesturing made them fun to have conversations with. Kimin moved constantly, shifting her feet from the floor, to under her, back to the floor, crossing and uncrossing her ankles, leaning forward in her seat, leaning back, and stretching her legs out. Everett found the quality endearing. Jeremiah also seemed to be moving all of the time, but in small, controlled movements. Kabe exuded a natural energy and athleticism.

Everett turned his attention inward. At times, he had difficulty sitting still when he was bored, and he could experience bursts of energy that allowed him to read or study many hours past when his mother had gone to sleep, but he did not feel a great connection with this OVEREXCITABILITY and decided that he would have to think about it.

The students that *had* connected with the OE were talking excitedly about their ever present need for stimulation, for movement, and for opportunities to be active and to interact. Jeremiah was shyly telling Mr. Dodd about his experiences with this in his previous classroom. He was older than the other children and had been forced to control his impulses to move in order to display appropriate behavior for many years. A nervous tic had developed from trying to minimize his movements to conceal them.

Everett started when he realized that he was eavesdropping on the conversation and moved to Greta's side. When he mentioned that he had visited the Human and Animal Sciences Wing that morning, she enthusiastically described an organ transplant for an adult male panda that she had witnessed there. She explained that pandas had been on the brink of extinction when The School for Gifted Potentials had

119

started and that their survival had been a project of great importance to the first few groups of MASTERY students.

"Their efforts in the last one hundred years have led to a great resurgence in the wild Great Panda population," Greta told him.

Everett was about to respond when Mr. Dodd motioned everyone back to the center of the classroom.

"I hope that this was time well spent," he said with a kind smile in Greta and Everett's direction. "I look forward to our time together later today."

With that, the students were dismissed. In the past, Everett had taken a tour after his first class with Mr. Dodd, but with the schedule change that morning, he entered the hallway feeling uncertain about his destination.

Everett followed behind Sev, hopeful that he might be going on another tour, but quickly realized that he was being led to Sindra's office. He entered her office buzzing with questions about the Human and Animal Sciences Wing.

He could tell immediately that Sindra seemed uncomfortable and distracted. She made a few brief, awkward attempts at conversation, but they mostly sat in silence. Everett was used to her coaxing information out of him in her blundering but sincere manner, and he found himself feeling worried about his advisor.

Something must have really shaken her to change her behavior so drastically.

After a few failed attempts at conversation, Sindra finally dismissed him and told him sincerely that she hoped that he would have a great day.

He left feeling troubled and followed Sev to a snack break. He ordered a comforting cup of hot carrot juice with honey and milk and sat down to sip it. The comforting heat and sweetness soothed him for the first few sips as he pondered Sindra's strange behavior, but the drink soon brought back memories of his mother.

Belatedly, he realized that it was the very drink that she had fixed for him the night that he had received the letter that had brought him here. As he sipped the juice, he recalled the sad look in her eyes as she had seemed to soak up every minute with him.

Had she planned to leave him all along?

Fortunately, the sound of Kimin's voice from across the room shook him out of his line of thought. Kabe made his way over to Everett's table as the others got in line to order a snack.

Kimin and Sonniy giggled and chatted loudly as they waited in line to order refreshments. Greta and Jeremiah waited quietly just behind them. Everett was too far away to warn Jeremiah when he saw Dre and Jace push into the small group. The dark, cold liquid from their cups splashed all over the group. Jeremiah and Greta were hit the most.

Greta looked in horror at the right sleeve of her usually pristine uniform, which was now stained and dripping. She covered her face with her hands and fought back tears as Jace and Dre apologized for the "accident" with a sneer.

Greta's robot rolled forward and gently led her away.

Everett stood up angrily with his handsome face twisted into a scowl. He started to follow Jace and Dre to confront them, but stopped when a firm hand gripped his arm. He whipped his head around and saw that Kabe was holding him. He tried to jerk his arm away, but Kabe held fast and would not release him.

"Let go," Everett hissed, but Kabe shook his head and pulled Everett back down onto his seat as he lowered himself into a nearby chair.

"You can't take them on Everett," Kabe whispered forcefully. "There are too many of them. It will just make you a target, and they will keep harassing you even after your ORIENTATION is over."

"How do you know?" Everett responded suspiciously. "Did your *cousin* tell you that?"

"Don't be like them," Kabe replied, looking at Everett with pity. "Don't fall into the *us versus them* way of thinking. Yeah, Jace is my cousin, which means that I know his parents and his brother really well, but I don't know him at all. I do think that it must be hard for him to understand why his parents brought him here as a baby though. He probably needs to feel like he is extra-special so that he doesn't feel abandoned."

Kabe's wisdom continued to irritate Everett, and the word *abandoned* pricked him as well.

"Well, feeling *extra-special* shouldn't mean needing to hurt other people. What do they get out of making the new kids feel unwelcome and unwanted? You can make excuses for them, Kabe, but I am not

121

going to accept their behavior. I'm not going to stay out of their way so that I can get through my ORIENTATION and then be left alone. I will know that while they are leaving *me* alone, they are bullying someone new. That's not acceptable to me," he said.

Everett pushed away from the table with mixed emotions. He wanted to rush after Jace and Dre to tell them what he thought of them, until he realized that they would probably just get a good laugh out of it and then pick on his friends even more.

Sev found him pacing angrily as he tried to figure out what he should do about the *originals*. He looked into the robot's reflective eyes and, for a moment, he almost felt as if the machine looked sympathetic.

"Am I needed somewhere?" he asked resignedly.

"Your next destination is Mr. Elan's class, and you will be late if we do not depart at this time," Sev replied.

Everett shrugged as he moved down the hall behind his robot and walked into Mr. Elan's class with his shoulders slumped. Greta was already there and had a fresh uniform on, but the look on her face showed that she was still upset by what had happened.

Mr. Elan walked into the room with a bounce in his step, but stopped abruptly when he felt the tension in the air and let out a low whistle.

"Is there a problem that we need to discuss?" he asked as he looked around the room.

No one met his gaze. He waited for a while, but when he realized that no one was going to share the problem with him, he pressed forward.

"Okay," he said with a shrug. "I know that you spoke with Mr. Dodd about the PSYCHOMOTOR OVEREXCITABILITY earlier today. He said that Kimin, Sonniy, Jeremiah, and Kabe felt a connection with this OE. I would like to begin by showing you some of the tools that we have available for you to check out. Greta and Everett, you are welcome to check these out as well."

Mr. Elan gestured to the tools that he wanted them to try. There were shoes with bubbles of air trapped in the soles that allowed the wearer more movement while standing, cushions to sit on that served a similar purpose for sitting, and bands of varying tensions and strengths that could be fiddled with.

Kabe approached Mr. Elan to ask if something could be installed in his room that would allow him to be more physically active in the small space. A grin spread across the instructor's face as he began to think of possibilities.

With Kabe and Mr. Elan sketching out ideas for equipment that could be added to Kabe's room, the other students made their way over to look at the tools. Greta politely declined the offer to try them out, but Everett joined in with the other students as they experimented with the cushions and the bands. Kimin and Sonniy said that they would use the cushions during class so that they could decide before they left if they wanted them. Sonniy also checked out a short band and started playing with it immediately.

Kabe rejoined the group just as they began trying on shoes, and he and Jeremiah both checked out a pair immediately. Everett took them off right away because he disliked the slight rocking motion that he felt while wearing them.

"Now that we have some tools checked out, I would like for you to share what you've experienced with this OE, and then we can talk about some specific strategies for each of you. Please pay attention to each other. You might make some connections with what you hear," Mr. Elan said.

The students looked around at each other for a minute to see who would start. No one was surprised when Kimin offered to begin.

"Well, I guess you've probably noticed that I really like to talk. Not only do I really *like* to talk, I often feel like I *need* to talk. Like, it helps me process my thoughts. I also think better when I move around. If I have to sit completely still and stay quiet, I just don't think very well because I'm focusing so hard on keeping still. When I do my assignments at night, I usually record my thoughts rather than write them, and I usually walk around my room while I talk. That is why I *love* the SKEtch pad!" she finished. Kimin's hands moved expressively as she spoke, and she shifted positions twice. Sonniy nodded to show that she felt the same way.

Unexpectedly, Jeremiah spoke next.

"My parents died when I was ten," he began.

The importance of what he said caused a hush to fall over the room.

"My life was really happy when my parents were alive," he said with a shuddering breath. "They were both G and both had the

PSYCHOMOTOR OVEREXCITABILITY. We were always active as a family. None of us could sit still and there was never any need to. We walked around with our dinner plates and ate. We read books while standing up or while lying upside down with our feet on the wall. We went on long walks and discussed things like protons and solar storms and practiced speaking other languages. When they died, it was a complete shock. They were both structural engineers for the Intercontinental Oceanic Tunnel Transit System."

Jeremiah took a deep breath and swallowed. The other students remained quiet out of respect for the difficulty that he was having.

"They were building a new section on the system... there was an explosion..." Jeremiah trailed off as he stood up and paced the room.

"I was just leaving my EDUCATIONAL EXPERIENCES in a POD when the car was intercepted and redirected to the Social and Human Services building. They pulled me inside and told me the news. Just like that. My parents were dead. They had logged their final wishes for me in the CNI database when I was born and had not updated the information since that time. I was to go and live with my father's older brother Thomas, his wife Lethia, and their five children. They took me there immediately. Workers from the SAHS department went to my family's apartment and boxed up what they called *emotionally relevant items*, things like pictures, toys, and books, and sent them to my uncle's. They didn't even let me go home to decide what I needed to keep!"

He angrily slammed his fist into his hand.

"So there I was at my uncle's house, surrounded by cousins that I had never met. All I can say is, whatever I am, they are the exact opposite in every way. They didn't allow me to ask questions about my parents, or to grieve. Uncle Thomas mumbled something about putting the past aside so that we can make progress and the subject was never brought up again."

Jeremiah took a deep breath.

"My parents had allowed me to spend my time doing what I wanted and learning about what I wanted, but at my uncle's house, the day was broken into a rigid schedule. Because there were so many people living in a very small space, we spent a lot of our time cleaning and organizing, *contributing*, as my aunt liked to say. My uncle had never earned the G, although he did attend this school. I quickly gathered that my uncle struggles to complete things, like projects, books, and chores. My aunt spent a lot of her time monitoring him, encouraging him, and whenever possible, completing his work for him. He has a job as a data analyst, but he doesn't make very much money at it. My aunt had to be creative each month to meet our basic needs. Needless to say, they saw me as another mouth to feed and an unwelcome one at that. I heard them complaining that my parents made them my guardians without asking. I found out through eavesdropping that all of my parents' money had been left to me in a trust, and none had been set aside for my care in the case of their death. So I tried my best to help out, to not get in the way, and to not eat more than my share, but they were always mad at me about something," he said, his voice rising in agitation.

He clenched his fists as he paced the room.

"Mostly they got mad at me for my constant need to move. I wasn't even aware of my fidgeting, but it made my aunt and uncle nervous. I would sit at the table, almost unable to eat because I was trying so hard to keep my body still. It was the same at school. My teachers had the same expectation as my aunt and uncle; to be still was to be obedient. I had no relief. When I tested, they told me that this school had sent Observers to watch me at school several times, because both of my parents had been G, but I was dismissed from the pool of POTENTIALS because they could not observe any gifted CHARACTERISTICS when they watched me in class. I had to wait until I was fifteen, because you can sign yourself up for testing without a guardian's approval at fifteen. I sent in the paperwork the day that I turned fifteen and now here I am," he finished with a defeated shrug.

Jeremiah sat down looking emotionally exhausted. The class was silent as they carefully took in his story. Greta, as usual, was the first to offer comfort. She reached out shyly to squeeze Jeremiah's hand. Kabe reached over to pat him awkwardly on the shoulder. Mr. Elan removed his glasses and wiped his wet eyes. Kimin and Sonniy had linked arms at some point in the story and remained frozen that way.

Everett felt a powerful surge of empathy for Jeremiah. He had lost his parents and had spent the last five years with people that resented him, that would not allow him to grieve, and that did not accept him for who he was.

He got out of his seat to look out the window, feeling angry that anyone would be treated that way, and angry that the haven that Jeremiah had sought at the SFGP was an illusion. He had already been picked on by the *originals* several times that Everett was aware of and probably more than that.

Everett surprised everyone when he whirled around to address Mr. Elan angrily.

"You teachers keep telling us that this school is safe, that this school accepts and celebrates our gifted CHARACTERISTICS, that this school is better than our EDUCATIONAL EXPERIENCES. But it is not safe. My friends and I have all been bullied by the *originals*. I have told two adults that they have bullied us and neither of them helped me. Aren't you supposed to protect us?" he asked, his voice cracking with emotion.

Mr. Elan looked startled. Kimin and Sonniy's jaws dropped. Jeremiah looked pleased by Everett's outburst, and Greta and Kabe looked uncomfortable.

The silence stretched. No one spoke. Everett felt embarrassed at first but quickly grew angry and frustrated when no one responded. He spun on his heel and marched out of the classroom before Mr. Elan could react.

Sev trailed silently behind him.

Hot tears threatened to pour down Everett's face, but he gritted his teeth and forced them back. He navigated the empty hallway through a watery film, not sure where he was going.

Somehow, he made his way to the rec center. Other students were there and stared at him in surprise, but he charged over to the Nature Center without looking around. It was not until he was in the enclosure that he felt like he could breathe.

Sucking in a deep lungful of the humid, moldering air helped him relax as he wound his way over to the rock formation that he had found the day before. He squatted against it and took a few more deep breaths as he thought back to the steps that he had learned to manage his emotions.

He identified what he was feeling. Injustice. It wasn't right that the *originals* were allowed to treat others the way that they did. It was wrong for them to make new students feel unwelcome and unsafe.

The faculty seemed to be turning a blind eye to what was happening. Everett was convinced that they knew about the *originals*. He thought about what Jeremiah had gone through with his uncle and what he was going through now. It was just a different kind of

126

bullying. His empathy for the other boy made his heart pound and his stomach ache.

Identify the emotion. Sympathy. Anger. Helplessness.

He breathed deeply and willed his body to calm itself. Just as his body would begin to settle, a new image from Jeremiah's story would flash in his brain, and his stomach would clench again.

He breathed.

The image of Jeremiah huddled in the hallway flashed in his mind's eye.

He breathed.

He recalled the image of Jeremiah being pushed; liquid spilling all over his shirt.

He breathed.

I am feeling anger and frustration over Jeremiah's situation because it is wrong, Everett told himself. *I feel helpless because I have tried to reach out to my advisor and teachers to tell them about the situation and no one has helped us. It bothers me that the* originals *have gotten away with bullying with no repercussions.*

His pulse calmed and his need to breathe deeply lessened. As his anger faded, he felt weary and sat down with his back to the rock with his knees pulled up to his chest. He rested his elbows on his knees and pushed his hands into his hair. A new emotion washed over him.

Embarrassment.

He felt bad about his outburst.

What happened after I left? What are my friends thinking? he wondered.

A feeling of dread washed over him. Were there consequences at this school? He had stormed out of his class and had gone to the Nature Center without permission. Feeling panicked, he took a deep breath and held it until his lungs began to scream, then pushed the air out forcefully as he stood up.

He might as well go and find out.

Sev was parked right outside of the Nature Center, and Everett waited expectantly for the robot to speak.

Several moments passed before the robot said, "Your advisor has requested a meeting with you."

Everett bowed his head in acceptance and followed Sev as he silently led the way.

When he entered Sindra's office, he was surprised to find that she was not inside. He stood in the doorway for a moment, confused, until he saw a stack of papers sitting on his chair. As he moved closer, he saw that there was a note on top of the pile.

> *Dear Everett,*
>   *Sounds like an eventful morning. I am meeting with Mr. Elan right now. Please feel free to read the documents that I left while I am gone.*
>   *See you soon,*
>   *Sindra*

Everett was puzzled. He had expected her to be waiting for him with a stern lecture, or dismissal papers, or the Chancellor.

His eyes hovered on the papers. *I don't care what she left me to read,* he thought rebelliously. *I don't care about anything that happens at this school.*

His resolve not to look at them faltered when his eyes picked out the words **Landon Perry** printed in bold, dark letters. Everett was done in. He snatched up the papers, plopped into the chair, and realized that it was a collection of articles about the man that Everett was so curious about.

As he flipped through the stack, he realized that the pages were organized in descending order from the most recent articles about the Mars landing all the way back to his days as a student at The School for Gifted Potentials. The temptation to start in the past was strong, because Everett wanted to get some insight into how Landon had spent his days at the very school that Everett was now attending, but his curiosity about Landon and his crew landing on Mars compelled him to start at the top of the stack.

By the time that Sindra joined him, Everett was completely absorbed in what he was reading, so much so that he did not notice her arrival until she cleared her throat.

She smiled sympathetically as he struggled to tear himself away from what he was reading. For a moment, he looked at her blankly, not remembering that he was there because he had shouted at Mr. Elan and then left the classroom. The memory washed over him, and he flushed with embarrassment as he waited to hear what she had to say.

"I spoke with Mr. Elan," she began, stating the obvious because she did not know what else to say. "What you have brought up is a rather delicate subject that is difficult to handle for many reasons. The faculty at this school *is* aware that some of the children that started at this school at a very young age have banded together to form a group. They feel connected to each other because they have shared a similar experience, just as you have selected friends that you have connected with."

She paused to gather her thoughts, and Everett shifted angrily in his chair. He did feel a connection to Greta because they had similar interests and histories but that did not mean that he bullied other kids that were different. A picture of Kabe flashed in his mind, but he pushed it away, thinking that his competitive feelings toward the other boy were different from the way the *originals* treated him and his friends.

"I understand that there is more to this story Everett, so please bear with me. As I said, these children have formed a group because they share similar experiences and because they have grown up together and have known little else. We have seen an escalation of this type of behavior ever since the Chancellor changed the admissions policy at this school to only include children that could live here full-time. The option to live here full-time from infancy through adulthood has always been an option, and the children that start as infants have always tended to band together, while those that commuted or began living here at an older age used to form their own groups. I am sure that you saw similar groups form in your previous EDUCATIONAL EXPERIENCES," Sindra said.

She paused to allow him to think, but instead of thinking about what she had said about all children forming groups, her words, *ever since the Chancellor changed the admissions policy at this school to only include children that could live here full-time,* echoed in his mind. So the Chancellor had created this system? *He* was the reason that Everett could not attend this school, which he was beginning to admit was pretty amazing, and see his mother?

Sindra mistook the anger on his face for disagreement.

"Well, I am sure that if you reflect on what I said, you will find that most children find themselves as part of some kind of group. Mr. Elan said that the faculty is aware that this particular group of students has begun to call themselves the *originals*. However, you

129

alleged that these children have bullied you and your friends, and Mr. Elan said that this information is new to him."

Shocked, Everett burst out, "I don't believe that he didn't know!"

"Have you or your friends ever gone to a teacher to tell them what happened when you were bullied or hurt in some way?" Sindra asked with her eyebrows raised.

He was about to shout, *yes, of course we have,* when he realized that, as far as he knew, no one had. He remembered seeing Jeremiah huddled in the hallway after the *originals* had hurt him. Everett had gone back into the classroom while Jeremiah had stayed in the hall to talk to Mr. Dodd. Jeremiah had never told him what they had discussed, but he did remember the older boy pleading with him not to tell anyone else what had happened.

When Dre and Jace had spilled their drinks on Greta and Jeremiah, their robots had led them away to change, but he did not know if anyone had told an adult. He had suspected that the faculty knew about the bullying because of the uncomfortable looks they got on their faces whenever he said *originals.* Perhaps he had been wrong. Maybe they were just uncomfortable because the group had given themselves a title. Deep down, though, Everett felt that someone had to know that this was going on. Someone had allowed this situation to get out of hand.

To her credit, Sindra did not make Everett acknowledge that no one had spoken with an instructor and used his body language as his response.

"In the future, if there is another incident with a student that you feel is malicious, please get an adult involved. As for walking out of class, Mr. Elan was shocked and a trifle hurt, but he will excuse your actions this once. He hopes that in the future you will find a way to express your feelings with words, rather than storming away. He also left you an assignment for tonight," she finished.

She handed him one of the slim, metallic rectangles that he was now quite familiar with and he sighed. It seemed like the ground beneath him kept slipping away, and every time that he felt settled, a different section crumbled. Suddenly he felt very tired, lonely, and discouraged.

A single tear rolled down his cheek. It was hot, heavy, and painful to lose.

A variety of emotions filled Sindra's chest at the sight. Knowing what she now knew about the Chancellor's actions, she felt conflicted about the pain that the boy was going through. The Chancellor had made it seem as though it was in Everett's best interest to keep him in the dark about the terms of his enrollment, but because of the pain that he was in, she felt that he would benefit from hearing the real story. To know that his mother had not abandoned him, that she was just missing, and they had not known what else to do.

Although one part of Sindra felt that she should tell Everett about his mother, another part of her feared what the Chancellor would do if she broke his trust.

That fear caused her to look at the situation from a different perspective. If she told Everett that his mother was missing, he would worry and fret about where she was. He might want to try to find her, and Sindra knew that he would be unable to conduct his own search for her. Instead of telling him the truth, she frowned sympathetically and hoped that he did not see his story in her eyes.

Everett was too preoccupied to notice the emotions that were crossing his advisor's face. He felt helpless and drained. It felt like a page had been ripped from his life story before he'd had a chance to see it. He felt that if he could just read that page, to understand why this change had happened, that he could move forward.

He dropped his assignment in his pocket as he got up to leave and heard it clink against the sensory tool that he had borrowed. He ran his thumb up and down the cool metal. The friction of his finger on the metal calmed him somewhat, and he gave Sindra a small wave as he left her office.

The door closed just in time to cover her tears.

Acceptance

Sev ushered Everett down the hallway to get lunch as he told him that he was late and would have to eat in a hurry. Everett suddenly stopped as they approached the large dining space and the clamor of talking and laughing filled his ears.

If Sev could sigh, he would have as he stopped and faced Everett.

I'm not sure what to say to my friends, Everett realized.

Feeling cowardly, he asked the robot if there was anywhere else that he could eat other than his room. He knew that his dormitory was too far away to be an option.

Sev nodded.

"There is an outdoor eating space that is available to students. I will take you there," Sev replied.

Everett was excited by this turn of events. Some sunlight and fresh air was exactly what he needed. He ordered a blueberry and bran muffin for his meal and bit into it as he went outside.

He found himself on a veranda that had a few tables, a shaded overhang, and an open space where he could stand and soak in the sunlight. Sev had to remind him to eat his meal several times as he lost himself in the warm glow of the sun. A gentle breeze tickled the hair on his forehead, and he pushed the hair away with less sadness than he had in the past few days.

Being outside made him feel the connection that he had with his mother again, and this time the memory did not hurt as much. For the first time, he considered his mother's limited choices. Thinking about her words, she must have felt selfish for keeping him, for forcing him to participate in his remedial EDUCATIONAL EXPERIENCES so that she could enjoy time with him. She must have felt that it was the right thing to do to bring him here, so that he could understand himself better, make friends, and learn new things.

He sighed. It was all so complicated, but at least he was able to think about his mother and her choice with less pain and more trust in her intentions.

All too soon, Sev was telling him that it was time to go. He had missed the remainder of Mr. Elan's class and lunch with his friends.

Everett took one last moment to look around the outdoor space as he readied himself to go back inside. As he looked toward the northeast corner of the veranda, he thought he saw someone watching him through one of the windows. For a split second, he thought that it was his mother. Chills coursed down his spine and goose bumps pricked his arms as he took a step toward the apparition.

The figure, which was quite a distance away from him, moved away from the window at a leisurely pace. He shook his head. No doubt it had been a teacher who had paused to glance at the view outside as she walked down the hallway to her class. Still, the vision and the chills did not fade as fast as his logic wished them to.

He was so lost in the oddity of the experience that he forgot about his outburst and his embarrassment until he reached Mr. Dodd's classroom. He paused for a moment in the doorway, fearing that all eyes would be on him as he walked in.

That might have been the case if any of the students had been seated and quiet, but instead, he found Mr. Dodd and his classmates giggling as they balanced on one leg, touched their fingers to their noses, and tried to remain balanced. Everett shyly joined the group and tried to copy their movements. He was soon laughing as hard as his companions were and was growing tired from the exertion when Mr. Dodd finally waved them into chairs and dramatically mopped his brow with a cloth.

"That was a calming technique that you will find useful only in certain locations," he explained. "Try not to use it in crowded places or around people that would tease you for it. Although today it was a fun and silly activity, if you do it again with great focus and determination, it can both calm you and sharpen your concentration. I often use it when I am trying to complete a project and my mind starts to wander or I begin to procrastinate. Try it sometime on your own."

Mr. Dodd loudly blew his nose into his handkerchief, settled more comfortably into his chair, and smiled good-naturedly at the group.

"Now then, I understand that you discussed the PSYCHOMOTOR OE and your experiences with it in Mr. Elan's class. This morning we discussed that people with this OE often find themselves moving constantly. Mr. Elan told me that several of you shared stories about how your need to move has often gotten you into some trouble."

Everett shifted uncomfortably several times as he wondered if Mr. Dodd was going to bring up his outburst in Mr. Elan's class. He also noticed that the other students kept sneaking glances in his direction and figured that they were wondering the same thing.

"There are many ways that you can manage this need," Mr. Dodd continued. "I want to remind you that there are fewer restrictions at our school than in your previous EDUCATIONAL EXPERIENCES. You will rarely find yourself in a situation where an instructor is unable to make accommodations for your need to move. Of course, there are times, for safety reasons, such as in a science laboratory, when your movements might need to be restricted. So while you are fairly safe from limitations at the SFGP, there *will* be times in your life when you will be expected to control your movements. The following strategies can be used to calm and focus your mind and body. This is also particularly helpful for those of you with an EMOTIONAL OE, because this technique can also calm a racing heart or a churning stomach. I want each of you to make yourself uncomfortable. If you have the PSYCHOMOTOR OE, force yourself to become still. If you have the EMOTIONAL OE, try to conjure up an emotional memory that causes you discomfort."

He paused for a few moments to allow everyone to participate. Everett surprised himself by not selecting a memory about his mother or about his talk with the Chancellor. Instead, he found himself recalling the feeling of embarrassment that he had felt ever since he walked out of Mr. Elan's class. A hot flush spread over his face and his stomach began to tighten as he remembered the incident.

"Good. Now I am going to take you through a series of exercises to teach you how to control and calm yourself. Let's begin with a deep breath. As you inhale, I want you to imagine that you are drawing all of the air out of your body. Start with the air in your toes and slowly travel up your body. You are pulling the air out of your calves, your thighs, your stomach, your chest... your arms..."

Everett felt as though he was going to burst as he continued to draw a breath deeper and deeper out of his body.

"Breathe even deeper now to get the air out of your fingers, your neck, your head, your hair... Now exhale, and as you breathe out with all of your might, imagine yourself as a deflated balloon. All of the air has been pushed out of you. Your body is glad to be rid of it," Mr. Dodd said reassuringly.

Everett pushed the air out with all of his might and felt a little lightheaded, but also better somehow.

"Draw in new air with small breaths," Mr. Dodd continued. "Imagine that the air that you are breathing in feels light, fresh, and clean. Your body begins to expand with this air. You may even feel a little buoyant as the fresh, renewing air fills out your torso, your head, your arms, and finally, the very tips of your toes."

Everett was astounded. He felt calmer and more focused than he had in days, maybe in his life. He looked in awe at Mr. Dodd and felt jubilant, as if he now had a secret weapon. He knew that he could master this technique and felt that he would use it often.

Mr. Dodd led them through several more visualizations and explained that he was really just changing the imagery. The analogy changed to filling the body with sand and letting it pour out of the body like a sieve, to sunlight filling the body and melting away tension, and even to a deep sea dive where they struggled their way from the dark depths into the warm, buoyant shallows.

By the time that Mr. Dodd had led them through each of the examples, Everett could see that each student now wore a tranquil, almost meditative look on their face.

Mr. Dodd dismissed them with an understanding smile and a silver rectangle. Everett handed his to Sev as they began to move into the hallway. He was not sure if the group would want to walk with him to the rec center, so he waited unsurely for them to trickle out of the classroom with his hands shoved deep into his pockets.

Jeremiah surprised him when he embraced him in a wordless bear hug and then walked away. Kabe walked up to Everett next and patted him amiably on the shoulder before he jogged nimbly to catch up with Jeremiah.

Amazed, Everett looked at Kimin, Sonniy, and Greta. Kimin and Sonniy both gave him a light squeeze before they linked arms and skipped down the hall to the rec center.

That left him standing in the hallway with Greta. After an awkward silence, they walked down the hallway together.

"We talked about what happened," Greta said slowly. "There were some mixed feelings about what you did, about whether or not you handled the situation the right way, and about whether or not you should have brought it up with an instructor."

Everett waited for Greta to continue with his fists still shoved deep in his pockets. Greta stopped to face him.

"What we all *did* agree on was that you were very brave, that you were following your heart, and that you were trying to help

Jeremiah," Greta said with a smile. She gave him a gentle squeeze on his shoulder before she walked into the rec center alone.

Everett felt dazed, but also satisfied and relieved. He leaned against the wall for a few moments to let the information sink in. His friends were not angry with him, and although some might not have agreed with his actions, they all supported him and his intentions.

The deep calm that he had felt in Mr. Dodd's class returned, and he walked happily into the rec center with Sev trailing faithfully behind.

A Plan of Action

Everett respectfully ordered his meal as soon as he got back to his room that night and hid a smile when he sensed that Sev was pleased. He hopped into a hot, steamy shower as he waited for the food to arrive. There was not as much tension to wash away that night because the effects of the breathing exercises in Mr. Dodd's class still lingered. The wonderful feeling from spending time with Greta in the Nature Center also remained.

A smile came unbidden to his face as he recalled their conversation. While Greta knew a lot of facts about the plants and animals of the South American rain forest, Everett had a deeper understanding of the delicate interplay between plants and animals, the need for predators, and the effects of weather changes. She had shared her knowledge with him, and he had discussed these ideas with her.

Greta had been so interested in what he was telling her that she had made him promise to finish his thoughts on a video call. She had explained that he could not conduct an interactive video call during his ORIENTATION and could only leave a one minute recorded message, but she had also hinted that he could leave as many of those as he wanted.

His goofy grin lingered as he shuffled back to his room to eat the meal that had just arrived. Kimin had mentioned that a delivery time could be attached to orders, so he could appease Sev by ordering once he got in the room but could still take a shower to unwind before eating a hot meal. He savored each bite as he thought about his day.

It had been an eventful day, but he was at peace with the day's events. His embarrassment over his outburst in Mr. Elan's class had faded with his friends' support. The bear hug from Jeremiah had meant the most. He would have felt terrible if he had upset the other boy with his outburst, but in the end, it seemed as though Jeremiah appreciated his actions.

As he thought about ending up in Sindra's office because of his outburst, he recalled that he had left the articles about Landon Perry in her office. He smacked his hand to his forehead and asked Sev how he could get the articles back.

Sev responded by inserting a silver rectangle into the data port on Everett's wall. A video message from Sindra popped up. She had a wry smile on her face as she began speaking.

"I hope that your day progressed well after we met. You left your articles about Landon Perry behind, but based on how engrossed you were with them when I arrived, I will presume that you left them because you were distracted and not because you were disinterested. I had them scanned for you onto this drive, and I will retain the hard copies for you to look at if you need them. Have a restful night. I look forward to seeing you tomorrow."

Sindra signed off with a small wave, and a menu of media replaced her image. It contained a large collection of articles, which he had seen in her office, but in addition, there were videos, interviews, photos, and even a digital copy of Perry's autobiography.

Everett tingled with excitement and anticipation. He was about to select an article to view when Sev politely reminded him that he had several assignments that he needed to complete that night. Everett gritted his teeth, knowing that he would have to prioritize his time.

Mr. Elan had left him an assignment to complete for missing his class, and he also had an assignment from Mr. Dodd. On top of that, he wanted to be sure to make the time to leave the video messages for Greta.

I am feeling overwhelmed, he told himself as he felt his heart rate increasing. *I have a lot to do tonight, but I can do everything if I focus and prioritize.*

He felt himself relax and requested his SKEtch pad from his robot. Sev handed him the SKEtch pad along with the drives that held his assignments. He was about to insert the drive from Mr. Elan when he realized that he should leave Greta's video message first. If he had asked her to leave a video message for him, he knew that he would be anxiously waiting to receive it.

Sev showed him how to record the message and send it using the SKEtch pad. He thought about where their conversation had left off and composed his thoughts.

"Hi Greta. So we were talking about symbiosis, which is how some plants and animals survive with the help of another. Parasites are organisms that are helped by another organism to survive, but they hurt that organism in the process. Mutualism occurs when two organisms help each other survive. Commensalism happens when one organism helps another organism survive, but is not helped or hurt by the relationship."

The one minute mark was up, and the recording stopped. Everett sent it to Greta as he wondered if he should say more. When he realized that he was chewing on his stylus as he waited, he sheepishly placed it on the table and got up to walk around.

He was about to switch gears and insert Mr. Elan's drive when he heard ringing.

Excitedly, he hurried to push the accept button.

Greta's face appeared thoughtful as she greeted him.

"Thank you Everett. I guess I knew that some plants and animals survive with the help of others, but I didn't realize that there were different forms of that relationship. I will think about this tonight. I hope that you don't mind talking with me about it tomorrow. Good night!"

Everett smiled. He wished that they could go back and forth all night, but he realized that Greta was doing him a favor by cutting it short.

We have a mutualistic relationship, he thought with a smile.

After a moment of hesitation, he inserted Mr. Elan's drive and wondered if he would receive a scolding or an assignment.

Mr. Elan's face looked tired and a little downtrodden when it appeared on the screen. He rubbed the side of his face a few times before he spoke.

"Good evening Everett. I am recording this *after* speaking with your classmates and your advisor. Your friends told me a little about the problems that they've had with the *originals*. I say with complete honesty that this is the first time that I have heard that the *originals* bully new students. You threw out quite an accusation today. You implied that the entire faculty is aware of what the *originals* are doing to the new students and that we have done nothing to stop it. Having done nothing, you accuse us of being complicit. You say that you told several adults about what has been happening, however, when I spoke to Sindra and Ms. Rosenthal, they both said that you mentioned the *originals,* but you never said that they had bullied you," Mr. Elan said with his eyebrows raised.

Everett swallowed uncomfortably. It was true. He had brought up the *name* of the group, but had not given specific examples about what they had done. His embarrassment crept back.

141

"I am going to take you through a few problem solving steps, and I hope that you will use them in the future. When you are experiencing a problem, the first thing that I want you to do is *categorize* it. Does it endanger you, outrage you, irritate you, confuse you, or sadden you? Once you have fit it into a category, and you can create a new category if those do not fit, I want you to take some time to consider some *possible solutions* to the problem. Give yourself a few different options. As you think of a possible solution, filter it through some *criteria*. Does your solution hurt anyone? If you answer yes, discard that solution. Will your solution create a *new* problem? If your solution will cause a new problem for yourself or others, then discard it. Finally, will the solution actually *solve* the problem? If you said yes, and it is safe, and will not cause a new problem, then it is a great possible solution."

Mr. Elan gave Everett a few moments to process what he had said.

"If you found that more than one possible solution meets all of your criteria, now you have to select the solution that you want to try. Once you've tried a solution and it works, then hopefully your problem is solved. If it doesn't work, then try one of the other solutions that passed your criteria. Your assignment is to apply these steps to your current problem with the group of students that you call the *originals*. I will set aside some time to meet with you tomorrow to discuss the solutions that you create. Have a good evening," Mr. Elan said as the screen faded.

The silence in the room seemed deafening to Everett and his stomach twisted. As anxiety over the assignment began to creep up, he followed the now familiar practice of identifying his emotion and breathed deeply to calm his physical reaction to it.

Everett sighed as he settled into his chair and activated his SKEtch pad. As usual, his instructors had great advice on ways to deal with his reactions. He activated a brain bridge and wrote *the* originals *have been harassing my friends and me just because we are new* in the center. After thinking for a moment, he created a bridge for each *feasible solution*. He wrote *turn them into the Chancellor for possible punishment, retaliate and do to them what they have done to us,* and *go to an adult to report each and every incident.* Smiling, he added *program our robots to react to the assaults by running them over,* and *stand up to them together and let them know that we won't be bullied.*

142

His favorite solutions were *retaliate and do to them what they have done to us,* and *program our robots to react to the assaults by running them over.* A sense of satisfaction coursed through him as he pictured them, but he knew that they did not fit the criteria for not hurting others.

Talking to the Chancellor would be his last choice because he did not want to see the man responsible for creating the policy that kept him from going to this school and seeing his mother. He decided that he would share *go to an adult for support and report each and every incident,* and *stand up to them together and let them know that we won't be bullied* with Mr. Elan tomorrow.

He felt satisfied with his work and inserted Mr. Dodd's drive. He did not want to dwell on Mr. Elan's assignment any longer.

Mr. Dodd's kind face on the screen quickly brought his smile back.

"Hello Everett. We discussed some breathing techniques that can help you calm yourself when you are upset or when you need to focus your body and your brain. I showed you several different methods in class. Your assignment is to create your *own* images for the visualization technique. You will calm yourself even faster if you use an image that *you* create. I hope that you enjoy your work," Mr. Dodd said with a smile.

A grin of relief split Everett's face. He jumped onto his bed and used the remote control to dim the lights so that he could relax. The assignment interested him, and he wanted to be creative.

His brain flicked through images of things that were relaxing to him. It was no surprise that they all involved nature. He pulled up images from excursions that he had gone on with his mother but was careful not to let the memories of his mother overwhelm him.

A swiftly running stream that bubbled and gurgled as it splashed over small rocks entered his mind first, followed by an image of a mighty waterfall that he and his mother had hiked up to. Once, he and his mother had hiked to a glen near twilight. Their movement had disturbed a group of small, white moths. They had floated up from the tall grasses and had surrounded Everett and his mother for a few magical moments. Their soft whirring wings had created a gentle vibration in the air, and they had seemed to dance and flit like magical fairies. They had only stayed briefly, but the image had come to

Everett many times since it had happened, and it always brought a sense of calm.

All three images were soothing, and he decided to use them all. To begin his assignment, he pictured himself as a rock submerged just under the rapidly moving stream. He imagined the cold rush of water running through him, filling his limbs, his torso, and his head. He imagined the water pulling the tension and stress out of him and swiftly carrying it away from his body. After the visualization, he felt lighter and full of energy.

I will practice the waterfall tomorrow night after class and the moths the following night, he decided.

He got off of his bed because he was not tired and recalled the disk that contained the media about Landon Perry. After fumbling to find the drive, he eagerly inserted it and found the article that he had been reading in Sindra's office.

Everett managed to get through all of the articles and videos related to Landon's most recent Mars landing that night before he fell asleep midsentence.

An Unexpected Visitor

The next morning, Everett ate and dressed quickly. He had slept deeply and felt almost anxious to get going that day. His eagerness deflated somewhat when Sev announced that they would be visiting with Mr. Elan right away.

He followed Sev absentmindedly as he thought about the information that he had read the night before about Landon. His discoveries on Mars were so exciting. It seemed that he was an essential member of the crew and had been called on several times to find solutions to minor emergencies that the crew had experienced.

Everett blinked a few times when he found himself outside. As his head cleared of thoughts about Landon Perry and he looked around, he realized that Mr. Elan was seated at a table on the outdoor patio that Everett had eaten on the day before.

Mr. Elan waved Everett over to his table.

Unsure of Mr. Elan now that he was alone with him, Everett sat at the edge of his seat with his hands in his pocket. Mr. Elan put him more at ease with a gentle smile.

"I hope that you took some time last night to go through the problem solving process and that you have a few solutions to discuss," he said kindly.

Everett nodded and shyly told his instructor about the process that he had followed, the solutions that he had discarded and why, and ended with the final solutions that he had decided fit the criteria.

Mr. Elan looked pleased and told Everett that he had done well.

"So, of the two choices that you brought to me, which one will you try first?" he asked.

Everett squinted into the sunlight and took a moment to enjoy the gentle warmth of the sun and the soft breeze that caressed his face.

"I would like to try having my friends stand up to them with me, but I have to ask them first," he answered.

Mr. Elan nodded and said, "I think that it's more effective for kids to solve problems amongst themselves than it is to have an adult intervene. Adults can bring about a temporary truce, but the behaviors will usually start up again when an adult is not around. I think that you made the right choice, although I do want to remind you that it is important to keep me informed about what is happening, even if you don't want me to get involved. The safety of our students is a top priority with all of the staff here."

Everett smiled shyly and thanked his instructor as he got up to leave. As he turned to follow Sev off of the patio, Mr. Elan called his name.

He turned to look quizzically at Mr. Elan, who said kindly, "I'm glad to have you at our school."

Surprised, Everett nodded and followed Sev back inside.

Everett sped up when he realized that he was being led to Mr. Dodd's class. He hoped to get there early enough to share his idea with his friends before class started. He was disappointed to see that Mr. Dodd was already there, along with two new students, and was shocked to see that Sonniy and Kimin were missing.

The only available seat was next to Kabe, and as he slid into the chair he whispered, "Where are Sonniy and Kimin?"

Kabe irritated him when he merely shrugged. He tried to make eye contact with Jeremiah and Greta, but their heads were bent toward each other in a whispered conversation.

Frustrated, he got up to ask Mr. Dodd about his friends just as the instructor told the robots to hand out SKEtch pads. The robots whirred into action, and Everett sat down in a huff as Sev handed him his SKEtch pad. A scowl of irritation crossed his face as he activated it and pressed the button to pop up the privacy shield. Kabe noted this and turned his shoulder away from Everett, which made Everett regret his behavior.

Mr. Dodd tapped a few places on his SKEtch pad with his stylus and then worked his way over to the scattered students and sat down.

"Good morning. I would like to welcome CiCi and Hayden to our class. I have uploaded a questionnaire into the system for you to take. It asks questions about the IMAGINATIONAL OVEREXCITABILITY. CiCi and Hayden, I'll go over the OVEREXCITABILITIES with you once I show the others how to find the questionnaire," Mr. Dodd said reassuringly.

CiCi flashed a brilliant, sweet smile at the instructor, while Hayden stared at the wall, his dark eyes difficult to read. Everett followed Mr. Dodd's instructions about how to pull up the file on his SKEtch pad, but found his gaze wandering over to CiCi. She seemed young, probably five, and was a petite and pretty child. Her long, golden hair framed a pretty face with sparkling brown eyes and two dimples that appeared when she smiled.

Everett felt a deep and sudden connection to the little girl, although he could not identify why. He did not feel that way about Hayden. The boy looked like he was around Everett's age, but he was much smaller in size and stature. He had dark hair and eyes, a pale complexion, and seemed to have a permanent sneer on his angular face. He sat with his arms folded and stared pointedly at the wall. Wondering if the other boy was feeling like he had on his first day, Everett decided to try to welcome the other boy to the school.

As he turned his attention away from the new students to begin his assignment, he realized that he had forgotten to ask about Sonniy and Kimin. He got up again to ask but saw that Mr. Dodd had already pulled the new students aside to explain the OEs.

Frustrated, he sat back down and looked at the questionnaire. It was similar to the one that he had completed for Sindra and used *always, sometimes, rarely* and *never* to capture his reaction to each description.

It asked him about vivid mental images, intricate dreams, and ideas about inventions. It asked if he tended to mix truth and fiction, if he elaborated on the truth, and if he often spoke in metaphors.

His responses were mixed.

He answered *I create elaborate fantasies that I escape into to alleviate boredom,* with *often,* and *I take a true event and retell it with a mixture of fact and fictional events to make the event sound more dramatic to my audience* with *rarely.*

Truth had been an essential component in his relationship with his mother, or at least he had thought so, and he could not recall ever mixing fact with fiction. However, something about the statement tugged at his brain as if maybe he *had* done that but could not remember, so he decided to put *rarely* instead of *never.*

My dreams are vivid, with detailed and colored images, distinct sounds and smells, and have elaborate plot lines received an *always.*

His dreams were very detailed and he experienced them as if they were truly real. Occasionally, he woke up from a dream that was so intense that he had a difficult time separating it from reality.

I often find myself "off task" writing or drawing about what I am imagining rather than staying focused in class was difficult for Everett to answer. Certainly, he had always had the *impulse* to do that, but his mother had set very clear expectations about how he should behave at school.

He worried over that question for a while, not sure if he would be lying if he put *sometimes* because he had never actually done it. When he noticed that Mr. Dodd had finished talking with the new students, he got out of his chair and shyly moved to his instructor's side.

"Excuse me," he said softly and jumped a little as his teacher turned around with a smile.

Everett paused as he tried to think of a way to explain his question without talking about his mother.

"I'm having a difficult time answering some of these questions," he finally said. "A few of the descriptors are things that I have *wanted* to do, but I never actually did them. Should I only mark the ones that I have actually *done,* or can I mark them for the impulse that I felt as well?"

He turned his screen to show Mr. Dodd the question that he was struggling with. Mr. Dodd looked thoughtfully between the screen and Everett.

"Well," he said with surprise. "Everett, if you've had the impulse to draw or write in class when you were bored, but managed to keep the impulse under control, I commend you! It is difficult to have that much restraint at your age. I believe that it is fine for you to mark your answer with *sometimes* or *always.*"

Everett nodded and moved back to his seat to complete the questionnaire, unaware that his instructor's eyes followed him with a thoughtful expression on his kind face.

All too soon, it was time to put the SKEtch pads away. When the class groaned, Mr. Dodd reassured them that there would be more time spent that day on the IMAGINATIONAL OE.

Everett was torn between wanting to introduce himself to CiCi and needing to talk to his friends about his plan for the *originals.* Finally, he decided to introduce himself to her, show her to the rec center, and then talk to his friends.

Kabe beat him to CiCi's side and had already explained recreational time to her by the time that Everett joined them in the hallway. Hayden trailed disinterestedly behind them as they headed to the rec center. Everett shrugged and fell into step with Greta to ask her where Kimin and Sonniy had gone.

"They finished their ORIENTATION," she replied sadly.

Everett sighed. It was as he had feared. The friends that he had made would only be temporary. Soon they would all be in different classes.

Sensing his worry, Greta placed a gentle hand on his arm.

"Don't worry. We will still have recreational time together, we can eat together, *and* we can earn social time," she reassured him.

He smiled at her gratefully as they entered the rec center. Remembering his plan, he motioned to Greta, Jeremiah, and Kabe to follow him to a corner. CiCi followed Kabe over to the group, but Hayden hung back and now looked lost and abandoned. Everett made eye contact with him and motioned him over with a friendly smile, but Hayden shoved his hands into his pockets and turned away. Everett frowned at the other boy's reaction and then shrugged. At least he had tried.

"Hi," he began shyly.

The grand words that he had planned to say were lost, and he struggled to figure out how to start as his friends' kind faces stared at him expectantly.

"Welcome, CiCi, by the way. So Mr. Elan challenged me to find a solution to our problem with the *originals*," he said as his voice dropped to a whisper.

The others leaned in to hear him.

"I think that the *originals* get away with bullying the *transplants* because no one ever stands up to them," he said. "Well, I did, a little bit. I accidentally stepped on Jace's foot, and when he turned around and realized that I was a *transplant,* he got all puffed up to intimidate me. I didn't back down though, or look scared, and he looked a little shocked, like he didn't know what to do next. I think that we should stand up to the *originals* from now on. They might even stop messing with *all* of the *transplants* if we do."

The small group started to buzz with conversation. Greta quickly explained the problem with the *originals* to CiCi, while Jeremiah and Kabe discussed how the plan could work.

Greta addressed the group first.

"I appreciate your efforts to solve this problem Everett. It's a good idea, but I'm not sure that it will work. I'm thinking about when they poured their drinks on us. What could we have done differently? If we had gotten upset, they would have just laughed."

Jeremiah nodded in agreement.

149

"Well, *I* think that Everett is right," Kabe interjected. "When they poured those drinks on you, it was wrong of me to hold Everett back. He wanted to go up and say something to them. If I would have gone with him, and we would have all stood up to them together, maybe it would have helped. At the time, I was thinking that there *is* no stopping them and that we should just pay our dues and move on. But maybe we *will* be the first group of *transplants* to change how things work around here. I think that we should stand up to them together."

The tone of the conversation changed after Kabe's words, and everyone started to discuss how they would respond to the *originals* in the future. Everett exchanged a quick look with Kabe that thanked the other boy and was rewarded with a brief nod.

The group talked for a few more minutes and then agreed to split up to get a little of their rec time in.

Kabe and Jeremiah left to join in on a game that involved standing in front of a wall that shot out balls from random places. It seemed that they had to jump around to avoid being hit in order to play. Everett shook his head as he thought that the activity did not appeal to him. He felt restless and wondered if there were any outdoor spaces other than the Nature Center.

He headed to the outdoor portion of the room. In the past, he had always veered right to go into the Nature Center. An open air space to his left caught his attention and he turned toward it. Looking over his shoulder for Greta, he saw her leading CiCi into the Nature Center and gave her a small wave and a smile. The smile that she gave him in return was a bit regretful as she entered the enclosure without him.

Taking a deep breath of fresh air energized him, and he wiggled his arms. He felt freer now that he and his friends had made a plan.

A large climbing structure covered in ropes and artificial handholds dominated this section of the rec center. The peak of the structure was near the top of the third story of the building, and he felt an instant yearning to reach the summit. He climbed up several levels and used the ropes and handholds on the rocks to pull himself up to a rock ledge that allowed him to view the land around the school.

He perched on the ledge for several moments and allowed the sun and wind to infiltrate his senses before he had to climb down. When he was finally back on ground level, he looked up to the peak of the monolith and decided that one day, he would reach the top.

His friends were waiting for him just past the doorway of the rec center. CiCi and Greta were chatting quietly, while Kabe and Jeremiah hung together in friendly silence. Hayden had already left without the group.

Everett reminded them about their plan for the *originals* before their robots led them away from each other.

His thoughts were on the Mars landing as he walked down the hallway and through Sindra's office door. He stopped short when he saw the Chancellor sitting at Sindra's desk.

The Chancellor seemed to take up the entire room with his strong presence.

Everett stood in the doorway, unable to move. The man's presence frightened and disturbed him. He was beginning to adjust to his life here, but seeing the Chancellor brought back all of his confusion, resentment, and anger over the reasons that he was at the school.

The Chancellor motioned for Everett to sit in a chair. His smile was kind, but his eyes were steely and cold. Everett clenched his jaw as he sat on the edge of the chair and looked at the Chancellor with a mixture of distrust and defiance in his eyes.

"Good morning Everett. No doubt you were expecting your advisor. Don't worry, she will join us soon. I wanted a few moments alone with you to discuss the problem you have been having with some of the other students at our school," the Chancellor began.

Everett blinked. It took him a moment to realize that the Chancellor must be referring to his outburst in Mr. Elan's class. He looked the Chancellor in the eye, and to his surprise, he was not the first to look away.

"I was told that you are concerned about the behavior of some of the other students," the Chancellor continued. "You also accused the faculty of being aware that these students bullied you and as you claim, all of the new students to our school. However, it appears that none of your friends reported any incidences of bullying to the faculty here, and neither have you."

The Chancellor paused for emphasis and was about to begin talking again when Everett interjected, "I have already resolved that situation with Mr. Elan and my friends. I agreed to follow the problem solving process that Mr. Elan recommended, and I will keep him informed of all incidences in the future. I also shared the problem

151

solving strategy with my friends. Is that all that you wished to discuss?"

The Chancellor seemed to be at a momentary loss, but quickly gathered himself.

"Good, good," he said brusquely. "I just wanted to follow up on the progress of the matter. The safety of all of our students is a priority at our school."

"Yes, Mr. Elan said the same thing," Everett responded dryly.

His words hung between them for several moments before the Chancellor smoothed his goatee and stood up. He nodded briefly at Everett and then excused himself from the room.

Left alone for a moment, Everett exhaled forcibly. A private meeting with the Chancellor seemed strange. Either he had truly raised a concern with his accusation, or the Chancellor was keeping an eye on him. For some reason, he felt strongly that it was the latter, and a chill crept down his spine as he considered that.

Sindra entered to find him absently fingering the windowsill as he gazed outside with an unfocused stare. She was somewhat distraught by the Chancellor's visit. He had entered her office only moments before Everett's expected arrival and had asked her for a few moments alone with him. His demeanor had been similar to the night that he had asked her for discretion regarding Everett's unusual admission, and she wondered what he had said to the boy.

Not wanting to startle him, she cleared her throat as quietly as possible, but found that he still jumped at the noise.

"Hello Everett," she said softly. "I am sorry for the surprise. If I had known that the Chancellor wished to speak with you, I would have let you know ahead of time."

He did not leave the window, but he did turn to face her and accepted her apology with a small smile.

There was an awkward pause because neither of them knew what to say next.

Sindra finally broke the silence with a question.

"How was your meeting with Mr. Elan this morning?"

It took him a moment to process the question, because he was still shaken by the Chancellor's visit.

"It went well. I used his problem solving strategy and decided that I would stand up to the *originals* every time they do something to

152

me or my friends. I encouraged my friends to stand up to them as well," he told her.

Sindra nodded and fingered the edge of her desk as she said, "That is a great plan Everett. Would you like to discuss any questions that you have about any of your OVEREXCITABILITIES?"

He hesitated and then shook his head.

"No, at least, not right now," he said uncomfortably.

The silence between them stretched again.

"Does the Chancellor usually meet with new students?" he finally asked.

She jumped slightly at his question and then tried to cover her reaction with a wide smile.

"As you know, you are the first student that I have mentored. I am not sure what his common practices are," she said with false assurance.

The feeling that he could not fully trust his advisor crept back, and the back of his neck tingled. As soon as his session was over, he left her office without a backwards glance.

His friends were already seated for the mid-morning snack at their usual table at the back of the room. He still felt unsettled by the Chancellor's visit and the feeling that Sindra was hiding something from him. A cool glass of lemon juice and crushed basil over ice along with a bran and nut cookie renewed his strength. The soft sounds of his friends' chatter soothed him, and he allowed himself to lean back in his chair as he stretched his legs out in front of him.

He thought about the questionnaire that he had filled out in Mr. Dodd's class about the IMAGINATIONAL OE. A smile curved his lips as he recalled his answer to *I often create elaborate fantasies that I escape into to alleviate boredom* as he realized that he had not once escaped into a fantasy since his arrival at the SFGP. He had to admit that the fast pace, the variety of activities, and the interesting content of his classes had not given him a chance to feel bored.

His eyes followed Jeremiah as the older boy left the table to get a snack. He pondered the nagging feeling that he had gotten as he read, *I often take a true event and retell it with a mixture of fact and fictional events to make the event sound more dramatic to my audience.* Something still resonated within him when he thought about that statement, but he could not figure out what it was. He rolled his head around on his shoulders to ease the tension in his neck

153

and was startled when he saw that Jace and another *original* had cornered Jeremiah.

Jeremiah was backed against the wall with his snack crumpled in his hands. Everett sat up in his chair and drew his friends' attention to the scene. They looked around the table at each other and then stood up as a group and moved over to the three boys.

Kabe spoke first.

"Hey Jeremiah. We've been waiting for you to come back to the table. Is there a problem here?" Kabe asked.

The *originals* turned around to look at Kabe. A guilty look crossed Jace's face, while a sneer remained on the other boy's. Jace took a step back from Jeremiah and crossed his arms over his chest.

"No. There is no problem here," Jace said.

"Good," Kabe said and reached past Jace to grab Jeremiah's arm. "Let's go Jeremiah."

Kabe and Jeremiah left first, and Greta and CiCi followed.

Everett was the last to leave.

He waited until his friends were a fair distance away and then said, "I had a chat with the Chancellor about you today. Maybe you guys should find a new way to have fun."

Jace's arms dropped a little and the other boy's sneer faded somewhat. Everett stood his ground for a moment or two longer before he slowly turned and followed his friends.

As he left, he wondered what the *originals* would do to retaliate.

Triumph

Everett found his friends clustered in the hallway talking excitedly about what had happened. They all wanted to know what Everett had said to the other boys, but he politely declined to tell them.

He felt uncomfortable telling them that he had met with the Chancellor that morning. Something told him that none of them had or would see the Chancellor during their ORIENTATION, and he had no good answer for why the man was taking a special interest in him.

They walked into Mr. Elan's class still talking and settled into their seats. Hayden was already in the room and sat with his arms crossed over his chest and a defiant scowl on his face.

Mr. Elan walked in with a smile and quickly divided the students into two groups. The students faced each other and giggled with anticipation.

"This morning you filled out a questionnaire about the IMAGINATIONAL OE. We are going to talk about what the inner experience of this OE is like. Your dreams have more *intensity* and *depth* and can often seem real."

CiCi shyly raised her hand.

"CiCi, please feel free to speak freely in my class. You don't need to raise your hand. What is your question?" Mr. Elan said kindly.

"Well, I guess I thought that everyone had dreams. Are you saying that only some people do?" she asked.

Mr. Elan shook his head as he answered, "Everyone has dreams, CiCi, but the dreams of a person with this OE are more *intense*. The dreamer will also be more *aware* of their dreams and may remember them for a long time after they happen."

Everett nodded as he connected strongly to Mr. Elan's description.

"People with this OE often mix fiction with reality," Mr. Elan continued. "They picture things in great detail, both when awake and when asleep. You might feel sometimes that you think in *impressions* and *images* rather than in words. An imagination is a wonderful thing to have, and people with this OE are usually well entertained by the things that they think of! With this OE, you have to learn how to control your imagination, because sometimes you need to be able to focus on a task, and because it is important to be able to separate fiction from reality."

Hayden shifted in his chair as if he had never been more bored.

"The beauty of this OE is the way that you *experience* life. The challenges can be learning to communicate with others, as well as learning to separate fiction and reality. Today you will work with a partner to select one of the traits of the IMAGINATIONAL OE and then design a skit to show the benefits of the OE along with a managing strategy," Mr. Elan said with a smile.

Everett and Greta made eye contact to express their unease with the assignment. Everyone realized at about the same time that they needed a partner. Everett and Greta moved quickly to one another's side, and Kabe grabbed CiCi's hand, which left Jeremiah to work with Hayden. Greta gave him a sympathetic shrug.

After everyone was paired up, Mr. Elan said, "Those of you with a STRENGTH in PERFORMING ARTS will probably enjoy this the most, while those of you with the EMOTIONAL OE might feel worried about how others will judge you in this activity. I want to be sure that we all feel safe to work outside of our comfort zones. Please remember to stay positive with one another. I will give you some time to work with your partner to create a list of traits that are associated with this OE. After you have done that, I will help you select the one that you will show to the group so that we do not duplicate them."

Greta and Everett shrugged as their robots passed out their SKEtch pads. Mr. Elan showed them how to use the list function on the screen, although he said that they could also create a bridge. Everett and Greta agreed to try out the list feature.

"People with the IMAGINATIONAL OE tend to have vivid dreams," Greta offered shyly.

Everett nodded and they both wrote the words *vivid dreamers* at the top of the list.

"They also tend to mix truth with fiction," Everett added. "Maybe we can call them *story embellishers*."

Greta smiled and they added the words. They continued to throw out ideas to each other until they had written *vivid dreamers, story embellishers, architects of imaginary worlds,* and *metaphorical speakers.*

As they finished, Mr. Elan asked the partners to pull their chairs into a semi-circle in front of the board. He asked the class to share their thoughts about the characteristics of people with the IMAGINATIONAL OE and encouraged students to add to their charts as they listened. As Mr. Elan wrote the suggestions on the board, Everett added *inventive, think and dream in images,* and *think in impressions* to his list.

Mr. Elan stood back from the board to look at it and nodded.

"Great. Now I want to talk about how this OE can cause others to react. For example, if I am with Everett and we both see the same event, and I later hear him retell the story to Greta, but he makes the event sound different or more dramatic, what will I think about Everett?" he asked.

The class paused thoughtfully and then turned to discuss the question with each other. Everett suddenly realized what had been nagging at him about the questionnaire. He remembered his outburst to Mr. Elan and his accusation that the faculty knew that he and his friends had been bullied, when in reality he had only said the word *originals* to the adults that he had spoken to. *I often take a true event and retell it with a mixture of fact and fictional events to make the event sound more dramatic to my audience* now rang truer for Everett, at least for that event.

As the conversations began to wane, Mr. Elan asked them to find a new partner to create a skit with. Everett quickly latched on to CiCi, beating Jeremiah and Greta, who had both started toward the little girl. Shrugging, they turned to each other as partners, which left Kabe to partner with Hayden.

CiCi smiled sweetly at Everett, revealing the dimples on her cheeks. He suggested that they start at the top of the list and work their way down. She countered that they should start at the bottom and work their way up with a teasing smile.

Chuckling, he agreed and picked up his stylus.

They started with *think in impressions.* Everett understood this one on an intuitive level. He explained to CiCi that he often *knew* about things but could not fully explain them in words. They were just impressions in his mind that mixed with emotions and inferences that wrapped around the topic.

CiCi nodded and said, "It must be hard to explain yourself with words to other people when you don't always think in words."

"Yes!" Everett replied, a little loudly judging by the way that everyone looked up at him. "Yes. So a managing strategy might be to

157

find ways to change the impressions into words so that other people can understand you."

They shared a smile and tackled some of the others.

As they were completing their list, Mr. Elan crouched down to look at it and nodded with approval.

Vivid dreamers
Record dreams in a dream journal; learn to separate dreams from reality, especially in the case of vivid nightmares

Story embellishers
Sequence events clearly in your mind and retell an event using only the facts. Remember that you need to establish trust with your listener.

Architects of imaginary worlds
Make time to play in your imaginary world. Create a signal to get yourself out of your imaginary world when your attention should be in the present, like in class. Imagine a door or a lid or some other symbol that keeps you out of your fantasy for a while.

Speak in metaphors
Find a way to explain your thinking clearly to other people.

Inventive
Keep a journal; make sure to write down your ideas to play with at an appropriate time.

Think and dream in images and impressions
Find a way to interpret your images and impressions into words so that you can communicate clearly with others.

"Those are great strategies," he told them. "Would you be willing to act out *architects of imaginary worlds?*"

CiCi and Everett nodded unsurely and leaned in closer together to figure out a skit.

After giving the students some time to practice their skits, Mr. Elan asked them to join him at the front of the room. The nervous chatter died down as everyone settled into a chair.

"Let's remember to give out positive feedback to our presenters," Mr. Elan told the group. "I have only assigned three of the managing strategies to be acted out, but I am always available if you have further questions about this OE. Let's start with Kabe and Hayden."

Kabe bounced out of his chair to stand at the front of the room. Hayden took a long time to ease out his chair and joined his partner with a reluctant scowl on his face.

"We are going to show you *vivid dreamers*," Kabe announced.

He looked expectantly at his partner, who rolled his eyes before he pretended to be asleep.

"Hayden is sleeping," Kabe began. "Because of the IMAGINATIONAL OE, he is dreaming in vivid detail, with color and sounds. He is touching something in his dream and actually feels the sensation. He is experiencing intense emotions about what is happening."

Kabe paused expectantly, and after a moment of hesitation, Hayden began to thrash around.

"Not *all* dreams that people with this OE have are positive," Kabe warned. "Remember that there is a *range* and *intensity* with each OE. These people often have nightmares that are intense and feel real. When you wake up from a dream, if you have this OE, your heart might be racing if it was a nightmare, or you may have lingering euphoria if it was a positive dream. The emotions that you felt and the images that you saw may stay with you for a long time."

Kabe handed Hayden a SKEtch pad.

"If you have this OE, we recommend that you write down your dreams when you wake up. This can help you keep track of what your brain is creating and might also help you identify patterns in your dreams," Kabe said, nudging his partner to remind him to pretend to write.

Kabe finished with a shrug and a bow. Hayden got off of the floor and returned to his seat without acknowledging the clapping audience.

Everett thought that Kabe had handled working with such a reluctant partner very well. He did not think that he would have been as successful with Hayden.

Greta and Jeremiah stood up next and shyly announced that they would be talking about *speaking in metaphors.*

Jeremiah cleared his throat and said, "I am the wayward cloud that conceals the golden light of day."

Greta replied, "I'm not really sure what you mean. Can you please explain it to me?"

"Sure," Jeremiah replied somewhat stiffly. "I mean that I am in a bad mood today and might ruin everyone else's mood as well."

"Thank you," Greta responded.

The pair paused for so long that the audience, including Mr. Elan, began to applaud hesitantly. Greta flushed and waved her hands to stop the applause.

She looked up at Jeremiah, who finished with, "When you have the IMAGINATIONAL OE, you might find that people have a difficult time understanding what you mean when you use metaphors to express your thinking. You have to learn how to explain yourself with plain language, because it's important to be able to communicate well with others."

He bowed stiffly before he returned to his seat. Greta had already escaped to her chair and was staring fixedly at the wall with her cheeks flushed a bright crimson. The audience cheered and then quieted as CiCi and Everett went to the front of the room.

Trying not to laugh, Everett sat up on his knees to look like a robot with tracks. CiCi walked forward slowly, and Everett traveled behind her as smoothly as he could.

Using a robotic voice, he announced, "You are now at the rec center."

CiCi smiled dramatically and said, "At last, I can resume pretending to play in Nordia, my imaginative world, where I am a servant to the cruel Queen Manada."

She walked around and hummed happily for a few moments.

Everett announced, "It is time to go to Mr. Elan's class."

CiCi sighed and held up her hand as if she was holding an object.

"I must now leave Nordia to go to my class. I will close the door to my secret entrance and lock it with this key so that I am not tempted to go back until snack time," CiCi finished dramatically.

She giggled and curtsied and received a standing ovation.

"We were showing that you have to train yourself to "put away" your fantasies when you have to focus on other things but that it is also important to allow yourself time to enjoy your imagination whenever possible," Everett added to complete their presentation.

Everett hugged CiCi's shoulders as they headed back to their seats. Mr. Elan smiled broadly and thanked them all for their performances as he dismissed them.

160

The students walked out discussing the performances and what they had learned, but Everett hung back for a moment.

"Excuse me, Mr. Elan?" he said.

His instructor turned around with a polite smile on his face.

"I just wanted to say... that I can see now that I embellished the truth a little when I said that I had told adults that I had been bullied. I do want you to know that when I said it, I truly believed that I *had* asked for help. I wasn't trying to be dramatic or to lie," Everett said.

Mr. Elan placed a reassuring hand on his shoulder.

"I know that Everett. That's why we talk about our OEs and how to manage them. Hopefully, from now on you'll be better equipped to evaluate what you are saying and will make sure that you are selecting only the truth to retell," Mr. Elan said.

Everett nodded with an impish smile and said, "I'll definitely try."

He caught up to his friends just as they were making their meal choices. He told them about the outdoor patio and they happily agreed to try it out. They grabbed their meals and their drinks and settled themselves in the sunniest spot on the patio. It felt incredible to be a part of the group as they laughed and talked and teased each other.

They headed to Mr. Dodd's class with light steps and cheerful smiles. Their mood changed when they saw a small group of *originals* coming toward them from the opposite direction. They pulled tighter together and prepared for a confrontation.

To everyone's surprise, the *originals* hurried past them without making eye contact. They collectively exhaled and shared amazed smiles. Had standing up to Jace that morning really worked?

Elated at this turn of events, they entered Mr. Dodd's classroom, not sure what to expect.

Mr. Dodd was not in the room, but two large pieces of paper were on the floor with a pair of scissors. A message was on the board.

Good afternoon. You cannot speak. You must divide into teams. Each team must cut the paper into a circle that is large enough to hold the people of the group if they are standing shoulder to shoulder but should not have any slack. There can be no breaks in the circle,

161

and everyone on the team must participate. You have ten minutes to complete this activity.

The students looked at each other silently with varying expressions on their faces. It did not surprise anyone that Greta moved quietly to Everett's side or that Jeremiah moved to stand behind Kabe. CiCi debated for a moment and then stepped over to Everett's team, which left Hayden to move disinterestedly to Kabe's.

Kabe and Everett immediately set to work and guided their teams silently as they each approached the problem a different way. A lot of gesturing and nodding occurred before the first scissor cut was made in each team.

Everett's team cut a hole in the center that was large enough for the first person to get into and then cut a little more of the paper for each person as they squeezed in. Once they had the inside of the circle done, they stepped out to cut around the outside to create a giant O. Triumphantly, they stepped back inside and waited.

Kabe gestured for the boys to lie down on the paper in a circle with their heads pointing inward. They passed the scissors around and each stabbed the paper with the scissors at each shoulder so that they had a rough outline of a circle. Then they cut out the inner circle and stepped inside. Jeremiah noticed that the other team had cut around the outside as well and gestured to his team to show them the final step. Kabe stepped out of the circle as Jeremiah and Hayden held it up and trimmed the edges before rejoining his team.

The students waited expectantly for Mr. Dodd to join them with the paper O draped around their shoulders. Just as the children began to shift uncomfortably, he walked in and whistled appreciatively. He congratulated his students and told them that they could get out of their circles and join him on the floor.

"Today's activity was designed to find the students that show a STRENGTH in LEADERSHIP. Remember that it is rare to show all of the CHARACTERISTICS and the OEs, so you should not expect to demonstrate all of them. If you have this CHARACTERISTIC, your peers will often look to you for guidance to organize a solution when a challenge presents itself. You will have the ability to recognize the strengths of the people that you are working with and will delegate responsibilities. You won't give yourself the main role in a task if you feel that one of your companions has a greater STRENGTH in an area than you do. You can listen to all ideas given and can articulate them, organize them, and coordinate their implementation."

Mr. Dodd struggled to stand and gestured for the students to follow suit.

"I would like you to reflect on which role you took in this activity. Even if you were not the main leader in the activity, you might have shown some leadership qualities. I hope that you have a wonderful evening," he said as he dismissed them with a friendly wave.

Still feeling a rush of adrenaline from the activity in Mr. Dodd's class, Everett again chose the climbing structure for his activity during rec time. He thought about his role in the activity, as Mr. Dodd had suggested, and realized that he had been selected to lead his group by Greta and CiCi. He had never worked in a group like that before, but it had felt natural to take the lead. The feeling of elation lingered as he climbed, and he managed to make it halfway up the structure before Sev came to collect him.

After a refreshing shower and an indulgent meal of comfort foods, Everett stretched out on his bed to try out the relaxation technique that he had learned the day before. This time he let himself visualize the powerful waterfall that he had hiked up to with his mother. He imagined that he was standing below it and that the rushing water entered his body at his head and pushed out all of his tension and weariness. Similar to the night before, he sat up after a few moments of visualization feeling renewed and energized.

He asked Sev if he had any assignments to complete and was surprised to find that none had been given. He paced around the room for a few moments to process this unusual turn of events. After a few moments, he asked Sev to get out his SKEtch pad. He was beginning to realize that the assignments that he had been given so far had been for his own learning and growth.

I shouldn't need someone to make me reflect on my learning, he realized.

His name flashed across the screen and he pulled up his brain bridge. He looked at the categories *friends, advisor, tour, classes, new understandings,* and *originals.* He tapped *new understandings* and the record button.

"I don't think that I experience the PSYCHOMOTOR OE," he began confidently. "It's obvious that Kimin, Kabe, Sonniy, and Jeremiah experience it. I see it in Kimin with her constant talking and moving. Kabe seems more at ease when he can move and talk, and Jeremiah seems like his OE is more of a release of pent up nervous energy. I think it's interesting that the same OE can express itself differently in different people."

He paused to think about the other topics that he had learned about.

"The IMAGINATIONAL OE does describe me in some ways. I definitely have vivid dreams. I have had flashbacks of something that happened in a dream, and I remember everything with such detail that it takes my brain a while to sort out that it was a dream and didn't really happen. I also have pretty elaborate fantasies. I've gotten good at looking like I am listening in class, even though I'm really thinking about something that is going on in my imagination."

Everett paused for a while and then tapped *friends*.

"Kimin and Sonniy finished their ORIENTATION already. It's hard for me to lose people after I've made a connection with them because of the EMOTIONAL OE. I never lost anyone that I cared about before I came here, and now I'm learning more about it than I like. I don't feel like I got to know Sonniy very well, but Kimin and I connected and I really did miss her today, even if I was too busy to notice it most of the time. I want to try to get to know CiCi better. We had fun working together today, and she seems like someone that I could be good friends with."

He stopped recording and got up to get a drink of water. As he thought back on everything that had happened that day, he realized that he had a lot to add to the *originals'* section. He felt too emotional to talk about the situation so he grabbed his stylus and jotted down a quick summary of the plan that he had worked out, his friends' agreement to it, and how it had worked for them to stand up to the *originals* when they were bullying Jeremiah.

He thought about adding the Chancellor's unexpected visit to the *originals'* section, but realized that he was not ready to think about the strange and disturbing encounter.

Feeling satisfied with his assignment, he decided to read more about Landon Perry and asked Sev to put the data on his SKEtch pad. After he was settled, he opened the file that contained articles about Landon's years as a MASTERY student at the SFGP.

He eagerly read article after article about Landon's accomplishments as a promising student in the area of biological sciences and environmental preservation. His eyes began to grow tired as he scrolled backward through time. He had begun to doze off as he reached the section that described how Landon and his friends had petitioned to open a science wing to pursue their MASTERY studies at the SFGP.

Sleepily, he read the names from the caption of the picture that he had seen in the hallway. Piper Long, Daniel Harring, Kayden Frost, Landon Perry, and Camilla Grey. The picture of the girl clutching Landon's arm, now identified as Camilla Grey by the caption, tugged at his sleepy mind as he scrolled to the last picture in the file.

That picture caused him to bolt upright.

The picture was a direct shot of Landon Perry and Camilla Grey smiling at the camera.

It was a picture of his mother.

Puzzling Pieces

Everett hardly slept that night. He was up and dressed before Sev switched out of sleep mode. The robot seemed startled to find Everett dressed and sitting quietly at his table.

"I need to speak with my advisor," he said in a deadly calm voice.

Sev led him down the silent hallway. It was early, so the halls were empty and his footsteps echoed strangely. Sev let him into Sindra's office with an assurance that she was on the way. He sat in a chair, perfectly still, as Sev moved to the corner.

Sindra entered in a harried fashion, breathless and disorganized. She dumped her belongings onto her desk and quickly sorted them out. With a sigh, she sat down in her chair and turned toward the window.

She let out a startled cry when she saw him sitting in the chair.

"Everett, I apologize. I did not know that you were in here. You are rather early this morning," she said breathlessly.

He nodded shortly.

"You said that I could come and look at the hard copies of the files that you sent me at any time. I would like to look at the hard copy of this picture," he said, trying to make his voice sound steady and natural.

He held out his SKEtch pad to show her the photograph of Landon and Camilla smiling into the camera. Sindra's brow furrowed in confusion, but she agreed to get the copy for him and hurried out.

Everett waited, scarcely breathing. He had convinced himself that it was possible that the digital copy of the picture was distorted, that he would see the hard copy and realize that he had been wrong. He held to that hope as he waited for Sindra, not allowing himself to begin thinking about what it would mean if Camilla Grey was his mother.

Sindra finally came back with a huge stack of papers in her hands. She rummaged through them quickly, her dark hair in her face, until she found the picture in question and handed it to him triumphantly. Everett pulled it toward himself slowly, knowing before he looked what the picture would show.

There she was, a smiling, beautiful, younger version of the mother that he knew. His eyes traced every outline of her face, and his fingers reached out to touch her cheek.

Hot, heavy tears poured from his eyes and merged to form a stream that dripped unnoticed onto his collar.

Sindra had been looking through the Perry papers on her desk and when she looked up, she was shocked to see that Everett had tears streaming down his face. Her first impulse was to ask him what was wrong, but her better judgment told her to give him some privacy.

She had barely glanced at the picture that she had handed him, not really wondering about its significance. Now she struggled to recollect what it had been of so that she could figure out why the boy looked so heartbroken.

She recalled that the photo had been of Landon and a girl smiling at the camera and searched through the remaining pictures to find another picture of the girl.

The picture of the groundbreaking ceremony caught her eye. She saw the profile of the girl clutching the arm of Landon Perry and read the names in the caption; Piper Long, Daniel Harring, Kayden Frost, Landon Perry, and Camilla Grey.

Camilla Grey.

Why was Everett so interested in her picture?

"Everett, you seem upset by the picture that you are holding. What does the Chancellor's sister mean to you?" she asked.

Everett's head snapped up.

"The Chancellor's sister?" he asked breathlessly.

"Camilla Grey," she said. "The Chancellor's younger sister. She is in the picture that you are holding. How do you know her?"

Everett stiffened and felt a deep chill of alarm pass through him. Suddenly he felt that nothing in his life had been real and that he could not trust anyone.

With all the control that he could muster, he shrugged and said as nonchalantly as he could, "I don't know who she is. I just really like this picture. Can I keep it?"

Sindra hesitated. His reaction seemed strange, but she nodded slowly and watched as he set the picture aside almost carelessly.

Everett sidetracked Sindra by telling her about how he and his friends had stood up to the *originals*. As he expected, the story of his success caused her to become almost ecstatic with joy, and she praised him repeatedly for his actions. She seemed to have forgotten about the picture.

168

She was still beaming and congratulating him as he left. He asked Sev to keep the picture and watched intently as the robot stowed it away. Sev announced that they would be taking a tour of the Architectural Engineering Wing. Everett nodded and forced himself to look excited as he followed the robot across a sky bridge, but his insides were churning with anger, betrayal, and fear.

It was one thing to think that his mother had abandoned him despite their agreement that he would sabotage the test because she regretted not letting him be challenged. It was another entirely to discover that she was a wholly different person.

He knew her as Mae Davidson, a chef with moderate talent, pay, and living quarters. She had no family and few friends. Her husband, Thomas Davidson, had died before Everett was born. Her life had been her son.

Her life had apparently been a work of fiction.

So she was Camilla Grey, the sister of the Chancellor of The School for Gifted Potentials. She had been friends with the legendary Landon Perry and had joined forces with him to create the Life and Natural Sciences Wing. She had been a MASTERY student, and it was entirely possible that she had earned the G. Maybe she had never gotten the tattoo. Maybe she had found a way to cover it up.

Why?

That question was the worst of all.

If she *was* Camilla Grey, what had caused her to abandon her identity, her family, and her friends, to raise her son in isolation and surround him with lies?

Everett nodded politely to Sev as he explained something about the model of the SFGP. The model was encased in a glass dome, and plaques and schematics that detailed how it had been designed and built were all around it. He noted with interest that the building looked like a spider because it had a central three-story body and eight, three-story wings branching out from it that were connected by glass paneled sky bridges. Sev pointed out the names of the architects of the building.

Ordinarily this history would have fascinated Everett, but it barely pulled his focus away from what he had just learned. He felt a shudder travel down his spine when his eyes rested on the Life and Natural Sciences Wing. Part of him wanted the whole story about his mother, but another part wanted to push what he had learned about her into the deepest, darkest place inside of him so that he could forget what he had uncovered.

Sev was leading him to another portion of the wing when Everett asked, "What do you know about Camilla Grey?"

It took the robot a moment to search his database for information.

"Camilla Grey was a MASTERY student at The School for Gifted Potentials. She is the half-sister of Chancellor Grey. She was enrolled as a full-time student when she was five years old. Camilla is credited with petitioning the board to add the Life and Natural Sciences Wing to the school. Her records show that she earned the G but never accepted the tattoo. She is currently in Southeast Asia working as a naturalist."

Everett smiled wryly. It seemed that only *he* knew better.

They finished the tour, but Everett could not have described the wing to anyone if they asked.

He entered Mr. Dodd's classroom a jumble of nerves and emotion. How could he concentrate on OVEREXCITABILITIES when he had just found out that his mother had lied to him about her entire identity?

Mr. Dodd was already addressing the other students when Everett slipped distractedly into a chair.

"...the INTELLECTUAL OVEREXCITABILITY is centered on the *intensity* of thought and a persistent need for mental stimulation. I like to compare it to the PSYCHOMOTOR OE, because just as a person with the PSYCHOMOTOR OE has an almost tirelessly active body, one with the INTELLECTUAL OE has an almost tirelessly active mind. I am sure you can imagine what it is like to have both!"

Kabe nodded slightly with a wry smile on his face.

"This OE is marked by a need to understand things, but not just academic things, because it also includes having a deep moral concern. If you have this OE, you *consider everything*; your actions, others' actions, and right versus wrong. Once you become interested in something, whether it is a topic that you want to study, or a problem in the world that you are concerned about, you are not satisfied until you reach an understanding of it."

CiCi raised her hand.

"Are you talking about intelligence?" she asked.

"No," Mr. Dodd replied with a smile. "The OE has to do with a drive to *understand*. You might become curious about something and invest hours reading about it, or conduct experiments, or do whatever

170

it takes to satisfy your curiosity. You can do this in an area of STRENGTH *or* weakness. That is different from intelligence. Intelligence is your *capacity* for learning. You can have intelligence in a strength area, such as math, but you may not have a *drive* to learn about math or any other topic."

CiCi nodded and rewarded Mr. Dodd with one of her dimpled smiles.

"Turn to a partner to share your thoughts on the difference between intelligence and the INTELLECTUAL OE," he instructed the class after he noticed several students exchange confused looks.

Everett scooted over to sit by Hayden after he recalled his vow to make an effort to get to know him. The other boy looked startled and crossed his arms to appear disinterested in listening to Everett.

"So the INTELLECTUAL OE is not the same thing as intelligence," Everett shared, "because the OE is more about *wanting to learn* about something than it is about *being able to learn*. I can be really good at, let's say algebra, but I may never have the *urge* to learn more about algebra than is required. However, if I have this OE, I might be terrible at speaking a foreign language, but I will still *push* myself to learn one, just because I'm interested in it and driven to learn it. So a gifted learner can have an advanced intelligence and multiple STRENGTHS, but not have the INTELLECTUAL OE."

Everett paused and waited for Hayden to respond. Unsure if the other boy was disinterested or confused, he added, "With intelligence people may learn things easily, but they may never have the *drive* to *understand*."

Hayden nodded and picked at the bottom of his shoe to show his lack of interest.

Everett shrugged. He had tried to communicate with Hayden and now had some time to himself. Feeling restless, he jumped up and walked to the window to look out.

His body jerked with surprise when he felt Mr. Dodd's presence next to him at the window.

"From your records it seems that you were an AVERAGE student before you came here. How did you feed your intellectual curiosity if you did not participate in your EDUCATIONAL EXPERIENCES?" Mr. Dodd asked him.

Everett swallowed. It felt like a genuine question. Mr. Dodd was not probing the way that Sindra had, merely looking for more

171

information about Everett's past to plump up his file. Now Everett understood why the records on him and his mother had been so sparse. It was because they were a great work of fiction. He shook his head to clear away his thoughts.

"My intellectual curiosity was fed by what I read in books and by what I observed about the world," he answered softly. "If I found something that was interesting to me, I got all of the books that I could find on the topic until I satisfied my curiosity. Many of the things that interest me relate to science and the natural world, so sometimes I designed an experiment to test something or I set up an observation station. Last year, I charted the stars in the sky every night for a year. I also wrote down weather patterns and major events that happened in the news for each day."

"What were you hoping to find?" Mr. Dodd asked curiously.

Everett shrugged as he answered, "I read that ancient cultures used the stars to predict things and I was looking for patterns. I think that I would need to repeat the study several more times in order to get the data that I was looking for. Do you think that I could find a way to do that here? I don't have a window in my room."

His teacher smiled conspiratorially and leaned closer.

"I think that I can arrange something like that. It sounded to me like you understand how the INTELLECTUAL OE and intelligence are related. How would you like to leave this class early and start another tour today? You would have to miss your recreational time," Mr. Dodd said.

Everett nodded eagerly. He did not feel that he could socialize with his friends at rec time anyway when his thoughts were so jumbled.

A tear pricked his eye as Mr. Dodd turned to convey the information to Sev. His instructor's act of kindness could not have come at a better time.

It was a relief to have some time alone to think about what he had discovered. He ambled after his robot, lost in miserable contemplation about his mother, until Sev's words caught his attention.

"….the Ashford Planetarium was donated to the SFGP forty years ago. Although it is used primarily for MASTERY students, Mr. Dodd told me that he might be able to arrange for you to use some of the data gathered at the planetarium to continue your study."

A huge smile cracked his face.

A tour of a real planetarium?

Data to continue his study?

His steps felt lighter and his chin lifted. He looked eagerly around the planetarium as they entered.

He lingered in the lobby for quite some time, looking at samples of moon rocks, meteors, and asteroids. Large photographs of celestial bodies, comets, and solar flares covered the walls.

Near the back of the lobby, he found a large photograph of the INTELLEX crew standing proudly in front of their space shuttle. Reproductions of the artifacts from Mars were displayed in front of the poster. He fingered them reverently until Sev ushered him forward. A MASTERY student met him at the door with a smile.

The young man led him through much of the facility and patiently answered his many questions. He allowed Everett to look into several telescopes and explained how to read the data on one of several hundred screens.

If Everett had doubted that he had the INTELLECTUAL OE, his tour would have settled the issue, because he felt like he could spend months learning in the planetarium without stopping. He regretfully waved good-bye to the older boy when Sev finally ushered him out of the planetarium.

The planetarium had stimulated his interest so much that it was not until he was rushing down the hallway with a snack clutched in his hand that he recalled the events of that morning.

To his great surprise, he actually felt a strange sense of relief to know that his mother had a more complicated story than he had once believed. He did feel a deep sense of betrayal about the lies that she had told him, but somehow knowing that she was a G, that she had attended this school, and that she had led such an interesting life fit better with the way that he knew her. Her façade as a chef had never fit with all of her knowledge about nature, or with her understanding of him and his need to learn.

Her fear of letting him attend this school now held new meaning. As Mae, the SFGP had been a frightful unknown, a way to separate her from her son. As Camilla, who had an intimate understanding of the SFGP, there was a fear that went beyond her separation from him.

What had she been afraid of?

What had changed her mind when she brought him here that had forced her leave him?

Everett recalled the strange moment that he had shared with his mother just before they had entered the SFGP.

"I thought that I was doing the right thing to keep you. Maybe all that you needed was ten years of love. Maybe now you need a challenge and an experience beyond what I can give you."

He had been so sure that she was wrong. Of course, he had never imagined that she would leave him, not after he had told her time and again that being with her was the most important thing to him. However, her words held a different meaning for him now.

He understood what she meant when she said that this school could provide a challenge and an experience beyond what she could give him. In just a handful of days, he had come to view himself in a way that he never had before. He not only understood himself as a gifted learner, but he was also getting to know himself as a friend and a leader.

These thoughts were still heavy on his mind as he entered Mr. Elan's class. He looked around for Greta and was shocked to find her missing.

Was it possible that he had been so distracted that he had not registered her absence in Mr. Dodd's class?

As he searched the room for her, he noted that Jeremiah was also missing. Hayden was sprawled listlessly in a chair, and Kabe was kindly listening to CiCi's chatter. Two new students that he had not noticed earlier occupied the remaining chairs. One appeared to be in her early teens and had long black hair that was twisted into braids. She had beautiful dark skin and sparkling brown eyes. The other was a boy who looked like he was in his late teens. His long blond hair was streaked with blue dye and he kept running his hands through it to get it to stand up taller.

Why didn't Greta say good-bye? She could have warned him that her ORIENTATION was ending. He realized with amazement that his own ORIENTATION would soon be at an end.

How could that be?

Mr. Elan walked in and asked the robots to hand out SKEtch pads. Everett took his SKEtch pad from Sev and turned it on, distracted by his thoughts about Greta.

174

"Hello again! I feel that the energy has changed slightly in the room with many of our friends no longer with us." Mr. Elan said and smiled sympathetically when CiCi and Kabe nodded.

"I just want to remind those of you with the EMOTIONAL OE to remember the strategies that we talked about for dealing with transitions and changes in relationships. Changes can be difficult to deal with, but remember that change also brings new experiences and new opportunities with it," Mr. Elan said softly as he patted Everett on the shoulder.

Everett thought for a moment about how his instructor's words related to Kimin and Greta. He realized that he would soon see his friends again for meals and that they could earn social time as well. His thoughts wandered to his mother.

Change also brings new experiences and new opportunities.

He knew that his mother had tried to tell him the same thing. That their relationship had to change so that he could grow, make new relationships, and fulfill his POTENTIAL.

A great sadness filled him for the choice that she had been forced to make. It was the right choice for his future, he knew now, but the most difficult for them both. A single tear slipped from his eye and coursed down his cheek. When he saw that CiCi had noticed his tear, he did not turn away from her. For the first time, he allowed a friend to see him express an emotion and was grateful for the kind smile that she directed his way.

Mr. Elan continued, "I want to share some managing strategies that work for the INTELLECTUAL OVEREXCITABILITY. I know that it might sound strange that this OE would need any managing strategies. With this OE you are driven to learn, you are able to concentrate for long periods of time on a project, or an invention, or an experiment, or tracking data… all of which are highly desirable qualities in our society."

He paused for a moment to allow his students to discuss what he had said. It *was* difficult to think of a reason that this OE would need a managing strategy. Although Mr. Dodd and Mr. Elan had done a great job of showing their students all of the positive aspects of each OE, Everett could not help but continue to see the difficult side of them. The INTELLECTUAL OE did not seem to have any drawbacks, so he was curious to find out what his instructor would say next.

"The INTELLECTUAL OE, like all of the OEs, is a wonderful quality to have. Your mind is constantly working, observing, questioning, and searching for answers. You are driven to work on something for as long as it takes, sometimes for a few months, and even for many years. You may have multiple interests and will need to learn how to *prioritize* your time, because you could become spread too thin on too many projects or have difficulty organizing the resources that you need to find the information that you are seeking. We will teach you how to create long-term and short-term goals, and will help you construct a prioritized timeline of what you should be doing along the way to accomplish your goal," Mr. Elan said.

Everett had a huge range of interests and would become intensely interested in a topic until he had learned everything about it that he could. He did not have the experience to know how to prioritize his learning and all of the projects that he wanted to start. His mother had helped him do that before, but now he had to learn how to do it himself.

He was excited by the challenge and eager to learn about goal setting. Everett was never short of ideas and goals.

"I am going to teach you how to use the goal setting tool on your SKEtch pad now," Mr. Elan said, holding his SKEtch pad up as an example. "Please find the tool in the upper right hand corner that looks like a line with arrows on either end. This is your *timeline*. Please open the tool."

Everett eagerly tapped the tool, and a line with tick marks on it filled the center of his screen. Mr. Elan showed them that they could rotate the line vertically, horizontally, or diagonally and allowed them to play with it for a moment to select the direction that suited them. Everett played with the line out of curiosity and then selected the horizontal option.

Mr. Elan showed them how to add words to each tick mark and then gave them time to select a long-term goal. He said that they should consider three to six months a long-term goal at this time, but they would soon be capable of setting much longer goals.

Everett tapped his stylus to his mouth as he thought about his goal. There was so much that he wanted to know about. He was also unsure about what was realistic at this school. Would he have access to the materials that he needed to conduct experiments or collect data or find books that held information about what he was interested in?

Mr. Elan saw his expression and made his way to Everett's side. Everett expressed his concerns, and Mr. Elan reassured him that the SFGP would most likely be able to accommodate most of his needs.

Everett smiled and tapped the typing tool. At the moment, his mother was the topic that he wanted to know more about. Now that he knew that she was somehow connected to Landon Perry, he typed *finish the Landon Perry file* at the end of the timeline.

His ORIENTATION was almost over. He had the feeling that his workload was going to increase rather dramatically once he began his academic content, so despite his desire to finish all of the files and movies and the autobiography, he knew that it would probably take him closer to six months to complete his goal than three.

Mr. Elan came by again to check his screen and nodded approvingly at the goal. Everett planned to finish the file with the articles and documents before he watched the videos and wanted to finish with the autobiography. Mr. Elan showed him how to expand and shrink the tick marks and how to change the order. He agreed with Everett that he would have a better idea of how to pace himself once he started his classes.

Mr. Elan ended the session by showing them how to add additional timelines to the same screen of varying lengths so that they could have multiple projects going at the same time.

Everett smiled thoughtfully as he realized that, of all of his OEs, it was this one that had always made him feel the most different from the other children that he knew, but also so connected to his mother.

It was the INTELLECTUAL OE that made the SFGP the haven for learning and discovery that he had only imagined existed before.

More Pieces to the Puzzle

As he followed his friends to eat, Everett realized that he was getting impatient for his academic classes to start. CiCi, Kabe, and Everett grabbed their meals and headed out to the patio as CiCi mentioned the two new students that had joined Mr. Dodd's class that morning. Everett had paid little attention to them. Kimin had been the one with the ability to meet others easily and pull them into the fold. His ORIENTATION was almost complete, and he did not feel inclined to make any more friends. He was simply too emotionally drained to put forth the effort.

The group was chatting happily as they walked into Mr. Dodd's classroom, but stopped short when they saw what was in the room. There was a multitude of costumes, musical instruments, pieces of artwork, enlarged pictures of students playing sports, and some equipment that looked vaguely familiar to Everett displayed along the four walls of the classroom.

Their instructor was already seated with the two new students and Hayden, who had a sardonic smile on his face as he listened to the girl earnestly express her thanks to Mr. Dodd for the opportunity to join the SFGP.

Mr. Dodd motioned them into chairs as they entered and welcomed them with a wide smile.

"Good afternoon. I see that you noticed the equipment that I brought in. Please have a seat so that we can chat for a moment before I give you time to explore it," Mr. Dodd said as he waved them closer.

Everett, Kabe, and CiCi reluctantly sat down as they looked longingly at the items around the room.

Chuckling, Mr. Dodd said, "Today we will explore the PSYCHOMOTOR ABILITY and the VISUAL and PERFORMING ARTS. Some of you are here because you have already been identified with outstanding POTENTIAL in one of these areas. Some of you have yet to discover if you have a STRENGTH in one of these areas. Those of you with the PSYCHOMOTOR ABILITY have a natural athletic ability. Not only are you energetic and enjoy sports, but you have a natural athleticism, coordination, and ability that helps you excel at athletic activities. In addition to a body that is capable of athletic prowess, you have an intellectual and intuitive understanding of the activities that you participate in. You also have the drive and persistence to

179

develop your STRENGTH and will push yourself to great achievements as you develop your abilities."

Despite an effort not to, Everett snuck a look in Kabe's direction. It seemed as though Mr. Dodd had just described him. Kabe had a natural athleticism, fluid movements, and rapid reflexes that Everett admired. He had not played a sport with him yet, but he predicted that it would take a lot of time and training on his part to be able to play a sport on a competitive level with the other boy. Jeremiah was different. Although he had the PSYCHOMOTOR OE and enjoyed playing sports, he was more awkward and less agile than Kabe.

Mr. Dodd motioned to the costumes and instruments as he continued.

"The VISUAL and PERFORMING ARTS are divided into the areas of art, music, and dramatics. Students with a STRENGTH in music enjoy music on many levels. They can play it, they can compose it, and they can pick out musical elements such as tone, pitch, and rhythm. Those with a STRENGTH in art have a great understanding of depth, perspective, and proportion, sometimes without even being formally instructed. They enjoy creating art and viewing art. Their creations are original and the artist may use a variety of media to create artwork, from oil paintings to three-dimensional sculptures."

Everett thought back to the charcoal drawing of the gargoyle that he had seen and knew that the artist must have had this STRENGTH.

"Finally, people with a STRENGTH in dramatics enjoy expressing themselves by taking on the role of another character, or reading with emotion, or evoking an emotion from an audience. They employ facial expressions, gestures, and variations in their voice and tone to convey their meaning or an emotion."

Everett felt a strange stirring as he heard this. His mother had never exposed him to any of these activities, but he felt drawn to Mr. Dodd's description of dramatics.

When he saw Everett perched on the edge of his seat, Mr. Dodd laughed and motioned his students out of their chairs. Kabe moved to the wall labeled PSYCHOMOTOR ABILITY, CiCi moved to the wall labeled ART, and he moved to the wall labeled DRAMATICS. He touched the costumes shyly and noticed that a SKEtch pad with a menu of media loaded onto it was next to each costume.

He fingered the rough tweed of a long overcoat and activated the video associated with it. A girl appeared and talked about playing the

180

part of an old man who lived on the streets. He had lost his wife and children and preferred to live among the birds in the park.

She showed how she had developed her character. He watched as her bubbly, smiling face transformed into a weary, haggard expression. Her voice changed as well as she read a few lines from the script. Everett was transfixed by her performance. She had become someone completely different. The rest of the video showed how she had used makeup, lighting, costumes, and set design to complete the character.

Tears pricked his eyes as he watched her final performance, and he knew that he wanted to be a part of that magic.

The class groaned and even complained when Mr. Dodd told them that their class time was over. He nodded understandingly and pointed out that they would all get a tour of the Arts Complex and would learn more about their options there.

Everett thought back to *his* tour of the Arts Complex as he followed Kabe and CiCi into the hallway. He remembered Dre and her message that he did not know enough about gifted kids and their learning needs to make judgments. Although he would never admit it to her, he now agreed.

The opportunities at this school were amazing and had opened his eyes to many parts of himself that he had not realized existed. His classes had highlighted why his learning needs were different and had been difficult to meet in his EDUCATIONAL EXPERIENCES.

He told Kabe and CiCi about the outdoor climbing structure as they headed to the rec center. Kabe was interested and agreed to check it out, but CiCi said that she had heard about a painting center and wanted to find it. The older boys found it and helped her into a smock before they headed outside.

Kabe's face lit up at the sight of the monolith before them, and he paced around the base of it for a moment to size it up. He found a rope dangling from the west side of the wall and used it to heft himself up the side.

Everett gritted his teeth as his competitive spirit welled up in him once again and mounted the structure from a section that had hand and foot holds to climb with. Both of the boys made it a quarter of the way up before their robots came to get them.

They paused with their hands on their knees, breathing heavily. Their eyes connected momentarily and they shared a brief smile, both

181

lit up with the fire and excitement of a challenge. They hurried down in a playful race, and Everett was pleased to find that his feet hit the ground a moment before Kabe's.

They headed over to the art center to get CiCi and oohed and awed over her painting. Everett had not expected much from CiCi because of her age, but he found that the scene that she had painted held an unexpected quality. It was a simple painting of a sunset over a small brook, but she had managed to set a tone of tranquility that he would never have been able to. Her robot informed her that it could be left in the center to dry and would be delivered to her room that evening.

She linked her arm through Kabe's and chatted happily with him about where she would hang it. Everett had never felt more normal as he followed his friends and knew that he belonged among these children.

I do not want you to be ashamed of your STRENGTHS *any longer,* his mother had told him.

His throat closed up as he thought, *I am not ashamed any longer Mother. I do belong here. I just wish that I could share it with you.*

Sindra was clearing off her desk to go home for the night when her fingers brushed the edge of the stack of papers that she had shown to Everett that morning. It had been a long day for Sindra because she was trying to keep track of several POTENTIALS from afar. It was difficult to be stationed at the school for so long, because she was used to traveling constantly in her position as an Observer.

The tears shed by her mentee that morning had been forgotten until she saw the picture that rested on top of the stack, the picture of the students that had petitioned for the Life and Natural Sciences Wing. She picked it up thoughtfully and pursed her lips.

His interest had been in the picture of Landon Perry and Camilla Grey, although he had acted as though neither of them meant anything to him. He had even looked surprised about the girl's name and her relationship to the Chancellor.

Sindra paced around the room as she stared at the picture.

What had caused such curiosity about the pair in Everett, and then such emotion? Her mentee was so confusing to her. He seemed so eager to learn, and yet he was still so guarded.

182

She turned her CNIpad back on and pulled up the file that she had saved on Perry. She scrolled quickly to the picture that she had allowed Everett to keep and studied the picture to find some clue to Everett's reaction.

The couple was young, smiling, and quite attractive. She tried to recall any information that she knew about the Chancellor's sister, but she knew very little about her, or Landon Perry for that matter. As she was about to shut off her CNIpad, something in Camilla's face caught her eye. She looked at the picture intently and then gasped. It was her eyes, her chin, her brow.

It was *Everett's* face.

Sindra's hand shook somewhat as she raised it to cover her mouth. Suddenly she felt afraid.

Could Everett's mother truly be *Camilla Grey*?

She shoved the CNIpad into her bag and made a call to a friend that she had not seen in quite a while.

Trying to keep her voice from quavering, she said, "Kara, this is Sindra. Would you be able to meet me for dinner?"

Sindra's head was spinning as she entered her apartment that evening. Kara had given her much to think about. She hoped that she had kept the conversation casual enough that her friend would not suspect that, of all of the people that she had casually inquired about, her interest had been only in Camilla and Landon.

According to Kara, Camilla and Landon had been a couple for many years and had parted ways after they completed their MASTERY studies. Camilla's older brother had just earned the coveted position of Chancellor and had immediately changed the residency requirement from optional to full-time residency *only*.

To protest his decree, Camilla had refused the tattoo that she had earned, but Landon had taken his, which was rumored to be the reason that Camilla had severed their relationship and left for Asia to work as a naturalist. Landon had entered the astronaut training program to work on the INTELLEX crew. His job was to find and document evidence of plant and animal life forms on Mars. The events would have taken place the year that Everett had been born, judging from his birth date.

183

She looked at the picture again, at Landon's long brown hair falling over his forehead and Camilla's hazel eyes and round chin. They must be Everett's parents.

The question was, *did Everett know?*

Final Questions

Everett laid down to complete his final visualization exercise. His breathing settled as he recalled the long hike up the mountainside. The gentle evening breeze had caressed his sweaty face and tousled his hair. He and his mother had stopped to catch their breath in a small clearing with waist high grasses. The golden sun was slanting over the clearing as the bottom of the sun had just begun to sink below the edge of the mountain. He and his mother had just shared a smile when the moths had fluttered to the top of the grasses. A trance-like feeling came over him as he recalled the light illuminating their transparent white wings from below. The sound of the soft whirring of their wings filled his ears, and he felt them surround his head for one magical moment. He allowed the moment to last longer in his visualization as he clung to the feelings of joy, comfort, and wonder that came to him every time that he recalled the moment.

He was surprised when a few tears spilled from his eyes as he sat up. He wiped his face and asked Sev to switch out of sleep mode so that he could retrieve his SKEtch pad. Accepting the SKEtch pad from the robot, he asked if he had received any assignments that day and was handed a slim, rectangular drive.

Mr. Elan appeared.

"You have learned that you have the INTELLECTUAL OE, and tonight you have the opportunity to look through some videos and articles about gifted people with the INTELLECTUAL OE that have used their moral concern and intellectual drive to help others. You will be able to keep this file, so please do not feel as though you must look at all of them in one night. I hope that you are inspired," Mr. Elan said as his image disappeared.

Sev showed Everett how to play the videos and how to zoom in on the text of the articles. Everett selected a video and paced a little as he watched it.

He quickly found himself overcome with tearful joy. It was about a gifted girl that was concerned about the plight of children that did not have access to schooling. She invented an earpiece that fit snugly into a person's ear that could transmit sound. It was wireless and used body heat to function and therefore did not need batteries.

The earpieces were given to children that worked in fields and factories for free and were set to their native language. The children that received them had access to educational lessons that were transmitted to the earpieces from a satellite at all hours of the day, so as they harvested grain or herded cattle or sewed clothes, they received a free education.

Her simple invention had begun to change the world, because as more and more people were educated, their quality of life improved dramatically. He was amazed at how this student had channeled her moral concern into an action that had changed the lives of thousands of people.

Everett was inspired by her story. He could sit around and feel terrible about how some things in the world were being handled, or he could use those feelings as motivation to think of ways to make positive changes. Eagerly, he watched the remaining videos and read a few articles. There were so many that he decided to stop for the night.

Yawning, he told Sev that he was ready for bed and was surprised when the robot informed him that he had one more message. Everett smothered a groan as he wondered if he had the energy for another assignment.

Mr. Dodd's face appeared on the screen. Everett was stunned when his instructor told him that he was reaching the end of his ORIENTATION. His assignment was to reflect on what he had learned and then prepare some questions that he had about any of the OEs and CHARACTERISTICS that he wanted answered the following day.

A sense of vertigo swept over him when Mr. Dodd informed him that he would not attend any classes the next day. Instead, he would have extended time with his mentor, with Mr. Dodd, and with Mr. Elan to discuss what he had learned and to plan out the structure of his next few weeks.

Mr. Dodd ended with a kind smile and said, "I look forward to seeing you tomorrow."

Everett's face furrowed into a concerned frown as the screen turned black.

So he was done with the schedule that he had finally grown accustomed to. It was time to finally begin the academic classes that he was ready for, but he would more than likely lose contact with the three adults that had supported him through this ordeal; Sindra, Mr. Elan, and Mr. Dodd.

Reluctantly, he turned on his SKEtch pad and set it to record.

186

"There are five OVEREXCITABILITIES and they all relate to the *range*, *depth*, and *awareness* that I have to my experiences. I experience the SENSUAL, EMOTIONAL, INTELLECTUAL, and IMAGINATIONAL OEs."

A strange feeling overwhelmed him, and a tear surprised him as it trickled down his face.

"I guess I feel *relieved* to know about the OEs. I can see the positive sides of all of them now and how they *enrich* my experiences. Although there is a negative side to each one, I would never trade how deeply they allow me to experience life. It feels amazing to see these qualities in myself and in my friends. It is the same with the CHARACTERISTICS. I belong at this school because of my GENERAL INTELLECTUAL ABILITY. I am interested in so many things, I love to learn, and I learn quickly. My love of reading, learning, thinking, and exploring ideas will be encouraged here, and I won't be held back anymore. I also have SPECIFIC ACADEMIC APTITUDES in reading and math. For once, my classes will be taught at my level, and I will be challenged. I even discovered that I have LEADERSHIP qualities. Mr. Dodd said that *the proof of being gifted is in everything we say and do.* This week, I understood myself better and better as we talked about the gifted CHARACTERISTICS."

Drumming his fingers on the table, he realized that he needed to come up with questions for his instructors.

"Thinking about the SENSUAL OE, I guess I still need to find out when I'll get those ear devices that will help me tune out background noises. The EMOTIONAL OE helps me understand why I have such a deep attachment to my mother and why I have become so attached to my mentor, my instructors, and my new friends. Following Mr. Elan's steps for thinking through my emotions to calm myself down has helped me a little this week, but I still want to know how to *really* deal with the feelings that I still feel about my mother leaving me here. The IMAGINATIONAL OE leads me to create fantasies, to daydream, and to have vivid dreams. I need to remember to start a dream journal. The INTELLECTUAL OE explains why I am so driven to learn about things. I think that the connections that I thought I made with the PSYCHOMOTOR OE were really this OE. I guess I should add the planetarium data to my timeline. I really do want to learn how to plan out goals and organize my time so that I can learn about all of the things that I'm interested in."

187

He wanted to add something about his mother, to forgive her for bringing him here, out loud. As his mouth began to form the words, however, an unexpected surge of bitterness overcame him and he clamped it shut.

He turned off the recording feature and crawled into bed. Even though he was exhausted, he had a difficult time falling asleep because he did not know what to expect now that his ORIENTATION was ending. He tossed and turned before he fell into a restless sleep.

Everett awoke the next morning with the strange sense that he had slept later than he had been allowed to on previous days. He relayed this feeling to Sev, who confirmed that his schedule would be more relaxed without classes. A grin spread across the boy's face as he put in an order for a large breakfast and went to take a hot shower. He had not been able to start his day in such a leisurely manner since being at home, and he felt invigorated as he sat down to eat his meal.

He chatted with Sev about whatever came to his mind as he ate, asked some questions that he knew the robot would be able to answer, and shared stories with him about the things that he had enjoyed about his ORIENTATION.

Sev led Everett down the hallway to Sindra's office for the last time. When he entered, she was gazing out of the window. She started a little when he cleared his throat and turned around to look at him with a sad smile on her face. He noticed with dismay that she had removed her posters. It gave the meeting a finality that he was unprepared for.

Frowning, he took a seat in the chair to cover up his sudden feelings of sadness and loss and fought against the lump in his throat.

A knot formed in her throat as well. He did not know how much she had come to admire him in the week that she had spent with him. He did not know that she worried about him, because she knew that his mother had not really given up her rights to him, and because she knew that Camilla Grey and Landon Perry were his parents. He did not know that she cared for the young boy who had fought so hard to appear AVERAGE, who now fought to appear as if his world had not collapsed around him.

188

The tears in her eyes spilled over at last. She wanted him to know that she cared for him, even though she could not quite tell him. Tears shone in his eyes as he looked back at her.

Sindra reached out to tousle the hair falling over his forehead and took a seat, blowing her nose so loudly that they were both forced to laugh.

"Well, Everett. You have been the most challenging POTENTIAL that I have ever discovered. You definitely made it difficult, but for *me*, it was worth it in the end. At our first meeting, you resented me for having found you. Do you feel that way now?" she asked.

Her question was earnest, and Everett gave himself some time to consider it.

If Sindra had never found him on that play pad, or if she had given up on him showing a STRENGTH, he could be at home with his mother at this very moment. He would have just sat through another boring week of classes that covered information that he already knew, but he would have had his mother each night. They would have read books together and talked about them, set up a science experiment, and discussed some topic that Everett wanted to know more about.

She would have held him and smoothed his hair off of his forehead. She would have told him at least ten times this week that she loved him and that he was special. Another lump closed up his throat.

Instead, he had spent the week learning how to function in a world that he never could have imagined existed. He had made friends that were smart and interesting and accepting. His instructors and his mentor had helped him think of himself in an entirely new way. He was no longer *different*. He had OEs, but so did his friends.

In this world, his sensitivity to noises and textures was normal. His need to learn was accepted and celebrated, and he would be taught how to manage his time and interests. He had a better understanding of his emotional connections to people and how to manage his emotional reactions. He realized that the imaginative world that he escaped into was something that he could control and was something that he should enjoy and appreciate.

He had been bullied by the *originals*, but he had also stood up to them. Somehow, he knew that their conflict would not be over once he had completed his ORIENTATION, but he also felt a strange confidence that he could handle the situation.

189

His interest in the Life and Natural Sciences Wing, the planetarium, and the PERFORMING ARTS gave him the impression that in addition to the work that he would receive in his academic classes, he would have plenty of goals to add to his timeline.

He looked Sindra in the eye as he carefully answered, "I think that there are many benefits to attending The School for Gifted Potentials. I also think that there are some things that could be changed to make it better, and I hope to take part in making those changes."

She looked gravely into his hazel eyes as she answered, "Everett, I believe that you will."

They finished their final meeting with the wrapping up of a few minor questions and details. Sindra would go back to her role as an Observer and would continue to try to find gifted children on play pads and in classrooms. She made a few promises to stay in touch and to check in on him every once in a while as they shook hands to say good-bye.

He was turning away from her when she grabbed his wrist. He looked back at her, startled, until he felt her take his hand between both of hers and apply a gentle squeeze.

He squeezed back and whispered, "Thank you Sindra."

A sense of heaviness at their parting filled him as Sev led him to get a snack. He enjoyed it in solace on the patio, realizing that he was eating at a different time than his friends, and wondered if this was how Kimin and Greta had spent their final day of ORIENTATION as well.

He was surprised when Mr. Elan joined him.

"Hello Everett," his instructor said as he sat down at the table. He took off his glasses and squinted into the sun as he wiped them off on his shirt. "I hope that you have some questions to ask me today."

Everett nodded.

"I understand the EMOTIONAL OE," he started. "I've used your managing strategies this week to think through what I am feeling and why I am feeling it. I have used deep breaths to control my physical reaction to emotions. Although those things have helped me calm down, I still feel like the strategy is *reactive*."

Mr. Elan nodded with understanding.

"I have a problem that I am still dealing with," Everett continued. "The breathing helps me calm down once I've *started* thinking about the problem, but it doesn't keep the thoughts and emotions from

190

coming back over and over again. How do I get over it so that the feelings don't come back?"

Mr. Elan took a moment to think and bit his lip as he thought.

He put his glasses back on as he answered, "Let me tell you a story Everett. I came to the SFGP as a student myself when I was eight. My parents had always wanted me to attend. They told me for as long as I could remember that attending this school would be the "start of my future". They talked about it constantly. At the time, it was optional to live here, although the school did try to convince people that living here is the most effective way for students to reach their full POTENTIAL. My parents signed me up for full-time residency. As I grew up here, although I fully enjoyed the camaraderie with my friends and the challenge of my academic classes, I sat up many nights thinking about my parents. I wondered if they missed me, if they regretted leaving me here, and if they would come and get me back someday. I went to find them as soon as I finished my MASTERY program. I wasn't sure how I would be received. Part of me wondered if they even remembered me. When I arrived at their home and my mother answered the door, she fell to her knees and cried. Great sobs racked her body as she held onto my hand. My father appeared behind her, and he also fell to his knees and wept. I was confused by their reaction and waited uncertainly until they composed themselves and invited me inside. I was shocked to see pictures of me all over the house. They told me that I had always been their most amazing treasure. *Losing you was the greatest sorrow of my life, but it was also my most selfless act, because I did what I believed was the very best thing for your life and your happiness,* my mother told me. I spent a few hours with them and talked with them about my experiences at school and the MASTERY path that had led me to earn the G. After I left, it took me a long time to process what my parents had said. They were almost strangers to me. Finally, I had to put myself in their shoes before I could understand the choice that they'd had to make. My mother's words, *my most selfless act,* helped me realize how much they had to love me in order to give me up."

He paused for a moment to let Everett think.

"I hope that helps you in some way," he finally said.

Everett nodded.

"Yes, Mr. Elan, I think it did," he replied softly.

191

He stood up as Mr. Elan did and shook his instructor's hand. Another knot formed in his throat, and he nodded a lot as Mr. Elan said good-bye because he did not trust himself to talk.

Sev took him to the rec center, and he found it nearly deserted. It was strange to roam around on a different schedule than his peers. He decided to take a walk through the Nature Center, because he wasn't in the mood to climb any mountains.

The process of changing out the biome had begun. There were no sounds of animal life, and a large section of the east side was fenced off. He found the stream and dipped his hand into the cool, running water. His hand rested in the water for a long time as he allowed his thoughts to drift, not wanting to think about anything specific. Finally, he realized that his hand had gone numb and stood up, shaking his hand to remove the water and get the blood flowing again.

After wandering around for a while with his hands in his pockets, he rejoined Sev.

"So what's next?" he asked.

Sev led him through a few hallways until they were in front of Mr. Dodd's classroom.

Everett stopped in the doorway, suddenly unsure if he would be able to say good-bye to this man. Everett had known very few adult males in his life, but he had connected deeply with Mr. Dodd. His kind smile and gentle way of helping Everett understand himself better had been the high points of Everett's ORIENTATION.

Tears streamed down Everett's face as Sev gently prodded him into the room. He saw Mr. Dodd waiting for him in a chair and sobbed harder when the kind man stood up and placed his arm around Everett's shoulders to give him a gentle squeeze. Everett's tears began to slow, and he snuffled and let out a few remaining sobs as Mr. Dodd handed him a tissue. He felt drained and sat down wearily across from Mr. Dodd.

He leaned forward with his elbows on his knees and looked down at the floor, afraid that his tears would start to flow again if he looked at Mr. Dodd.

"Well, Everett," Mr. Dodd said with a catch in his voice, "I say with all honesty that it has been an honor to get to know you. You have not said much this week, but everything that you have said has been honest, searching, and meaningful. I am sure that I learned as much from watching you as you did from listening to me."

The words hung between them for a few moments before Mr. Dodd cleared his throat. His voice became businesslike and merry.

"So I hope that you have a few questions for me. There must be something left that I can teach you," he said with a smile.

Everett nodded and began with the simplest question.

"When will I be fitted for the noise reduction implements?" he asked.

"Your appointment is at noon tomorrow in room SE600. I will send you a map of the location tonight," Mr. Dodd replied.

"That's okay, Sev can show me how to get there," Everett replied.

Mr. Dodd's brow furrowed.

"Oh, I mean Number Seventeen," Everett said with a small laugh.

"Everett, your robot will be leaving you this afternoon. Your final day of ORIENTATION will be a day of rest or exploration or reflection. You are expected to find your way around campus on your own now. Of course, the other students will be happy to assist you, and you will not be the only one that is trying to find your way," Mr. Dodd said reassuringly.

Everett's gaze flicked over to Sev. He pushed down the feeling of panic that was beginning to constrict his chest at the thought of losing his guide and his friend.

He looked back at Mr. Dodd and nodded as he tried to focus on what he needed to ask his instructor.

"How do you keep your IMAGINATIONAL OE from making a secret seem bigger and more dramatic than it really is?" he asked quietly.

Mr. Dodd looked surprised by the question and took a moment to answer it.

"I would just remember what you discussed with Mr. Elan about recognizing what is fact and what is fiction. If you think of something, and it is upsetting you, ask yourself, *is this truth or embellishment?* I would say that the majority of the time, if you have to ask, it is probably an embellishment or an exaggeration of the truth," Mr. Dodd answered.

That made great sense to Everett and he thanked Mr. Dodd for the suggestion. He knew that he would need to sort out and focus only on the facts that he knew about his mother.

It was time for Everett to leave, and he could only half-listen to Mr. Dodd as he explained that Everett would eat lunch in his room that afternoon. A schedule for his academic classes had already been loaded onto his SKEtch pad and he was supposed to review it after he ate lunch. If he was unsure about any of the classes or had any questions, he could leave a video message for Mr. Dodd.

After the schedule was finalized, Sev would give him a final tour to help him find his new classrooms and then would be reprogrammed to become the companion robot for a new student the following day.

Seeing Everett's face, Mr. Dodd reassured him that he was not the first student with the EMOTIONAL OE to become attached to one of the robots, which was why the companion robots had been designed to look more like machines than people. He reassured him that his evenings would soon be filled with opportunities for social time and video calls with friends, and his feelings of loneliness would soon fade.

Everett nodded thankfully and surprised himself by stepping forward to give Mr. Dodd a quick hug. His instructor expelled a surprised chuckle from deep within and clamped his hand on Everett's shoulder with a gentle squeeze.

He allowed himself a few more tears as he followed Sev back to his dormitory and fell onto the bed as soon as they entered the room. Within moments, he fell into a fitful nap caused by emotional exhaustion. When he awoke, he saw that Sev had ordered a meal for him and was surprised to find that it consisted of all of his favorite foods. He smiled gratefully as he ate and tried not to think about what he would do without his robot.

When he had eaten the last morsel, he asked Sev for his schedule. He was excited to find out what was planned for him.

Everett's Schedule

7am-9am	Earth Sciences; emphasis in Mathematics
9am-10am	Snack/Recreation/Study
10am-12pm	Life Sciences; emphasis on critical thinking
12pm-1pm	Lunch/Recreation/Study
1pm-2pm	Technical Writing; emphasis on description
2pm-3pm	Snack/Recreation/Study
3pm-4pm	Elective
4pm-5pm	CHARACTERISTICS of Gifted Seminar/Independent Study

Wow, he thought. *They certainly got my interests right. I also agree that technical writing is an area of weakness.*

194

"I can't believe that I get four hours of science every day!" he said aloud. "What does it mean by snack/recreation/study?"

"During your ORIENTATION, you were given specific amounts of time for each activity," Sev reminded him. "Now *you* will determine how long to spend on each activity. As you begin your academic studies, you may find that you are using the majority of that time to study since you will be learning the material at a faster pace and at a more challenging level than you are used to from your EDUCATIONAL EXPERIENCES. However, on some days, you will want to spend more time eating a snack with friends, and on other days, you might want to spend the majority of your time in the rec center. *You* will decide how to spend the time based on your needs."

Everett nodded thoughtfully. It seemed like a lot of responsibility to be trusted to manage his own time.

"How do I get to pick an elective?" he asked, feeling a sudden thrill as he said the word.

Sev handed him another disk, which he eagerly inserted into the data port in the wall.

Sindra's face filled the screen, which surprised Everett because he had expected to see Mr. Dodd.

"I have come to know you well enough this week to know that you are anxiously waiting to find out what your elective will be. You have been on many tours this week and have shared some of your interests with me and your instructors. Your elective will be flexible for many years. With the INTELLECTUAL OE, there will be times when you have many different interests at once, or you may pursue *one* interest for months or even years. For your first elective, I have given you an hour each day to study with a MASTERY student in the planetarium. You discussed continuing your study of the night sky with Mr. Dodd, and your mentor at the planetarium can help you get that data. You will be able to review this choice in two weeks. At that time, you will either continue the elective or select a new one. I sincerely hope that you are pleased with my choice. Farewell Everett," she finished softly.

Her understanding of him and his interests pleased him. She could not have selected a better elective for him. He had been wondering when he would get a chance to see the planetarium again and was excited that he would get to go there every day. It was also a relief to know that he would have some say in how long he spent taking an elective and in what the elective was. The CHARACTERISTICS of

Gifted Seminar confused him because he thought that he had already learned all about that topic.

"Why do I have a class about the CHARACTERISTICS of gifted? I thought I was done with my ORIENTATION because we had already covered everything," he told Sev.

"Your ORIENTATION covered an overview of the OEs and a few gifted CHARACTERISTICS," Sev replied. "There are many more to learn about, but the list is too extensive to cover in one week. Your seminar will be flexible. Sometimes you will learn with a large group, and sometimes your instructors will invite you to a small group discussion. At other times you will be released to work on an independent study."

Everett felt relieved, because he really did want to know more about himself and knew that there were several qualities that he recognized about himself that had not been covered.

Sev finalized the schedule and a map appeared on the screen that showed Everett how to navigate his way through the maze of hallways to find his classes. Sev volunteered to show Everett the way. They practiced the route several times, until Everett was leading Sev without looking at the map for assistance.

Everett was heading back toward his room when he realized that Sev was not following him.

The robot remained at the entrance to a sky bridge.

He went back to Sev's side and asked why he was not following him.

"I have completed my role as your companion robot. You are now independent in making your meal selections and in finding your way around the facility. In the future, you will receive updates on your schedule changes through a video message from one of your instructors."

Everett clenched his fists by his side, feeling helpless because he was not ready for Sev to leave.

"Thank you Sev… Number Seventeen. I could not have asked for a better companion robot to see me through this week. You have been kind, patient, and helpful to me throughout, no matter what my demeanor was. I wish that there was some way to thank you…" he trailed off, unsure if the robot was even able to understand the emotion that he was trying to express. "Thank you Sev," he said simply.

"Thank *you* Everett," Sev replied and slowly turned away.

Everett watched tearfully as Sev rolled away from him across the sky bridge. He knew that he would miss the robot and the companionship and security that he had brought.

So he had completed his ORIENTATION and would now begin his academic studies as a student at The School for Gifted Potentials. He had made friends, and a few enemies, as the Chancellor had promised.

He did not understand his mother's past or why she had concealed her identity from him, but his memories of her love and her passion for his learning held true. Her final words echoed in his mind as Sev disappeared down the long corridor.

There are a few things that I want you to remember. One, always know that I love you. There has not been a decision that I have made that has not been in your best interest. Two, remember to stay true to who you are. I do not want you to be ashamed of your STRENGTHS any longer. I want you to always be who you are, in any situation. Three, I want you to always know that I am here for you, even if I cannot be with you for a little while.

Everett smiled then, knowing that no matter what her name was, his mother had always been truthful about her love for him and her devotion to him. He knew that he would see her again.

You have some questions to answer, mother, but nonetheless, you have my love, he thought.

Throwing his shoulders back, he turned away from the receding robot and returned to his room with his heart full of sorrow, loss, and hope for the future.

Everett and his friends are fictional characters, but each exhibits some of the qualities found in gifted children. There are many definitions of giftedness, different cut-off scores, and different measures used to determine giftedness. I chose to focus on a definition of giftedness that describes a person with such extraordinary potential in one or more areas that their needs cannot be met in a regular educational setting.

The six traits of giftedness, General Intellectual Ability, Specific Academic Aptitude, Creative Thinking, Leadership, Psychomotor and Visual and Performing Arts, are categories that some states use in their definition of gifted and for the identification of gifted children, and were used to describe areas in which some gifted children show a strength. While those traits are often used to identify gifted children, they may still not explain to a gifted child (or adult) why they seem to experience life so differently than others, which is explained by the overexcitabilities.

The overexcitabilities described by Kazimierz Dabrowski have helped several generations of gifted people begin to understand some of the inner qualities that they have and how they react to their experiences. The overexcitabilities are a smaller piece of Dabrowski's overall Theory of Positive Disintegration and have been applied to highly gifted people by other theorists.

The following resources were used in researching this book:

Austega.com. Ed. David Farmer. 1995. Web. Mar. 2012. <http://www.austega.com/>. Used with permission.

SENG. Ed. Lisa Rivero. Supporting Emotional Needs of the Gifted, 2011. Web. 12 Jan. 2012. <http://www.sengifted.org/>. Used with permission.

Tillier,W. (2012). The Theory of Positive Disintegration. Website http://www.positivedisintegration.com. Used with permission.

Discussion Questions

1. Everett and his friends were all gifted, but had very different personalities, interests, and strengths. Which character did you identify with the most? Which character did you identify with the least?

2. In his EDUCATIONAL EXPERIENCES, Everett often found himself feeling isolated and bored. How did attending The School for Gifted Potentials change that?

3. Learning about the OVEREXCITABILITIES and CHARACTERISTICS was exciting for Everett. Do you feel like you learned something new about yourself while reading this book? Describe your *new understandings* about yourself.

4. Why do you think Everett felt competitive with Kabe but not with his other new friends?

5. How did Everett's feelings about Sindra change throughout the story? What did she do that made his feelings change?

6. Sindra knew that the Chancellor lied to Everett about his mother. Do you think she made the right choice when she decided to keep the information from Everett? Why or why not?

7. Predict what will happen now that Everett and his friends decided to stand up to the *originals* each time they are bullied.

8. The Chancellor is responsible for requiring students to live at the SFGP. Do you think that he made the right choice? Why or why not?

9. Find some examples of when Everett's EMOTIONAL OVEREXCITABILITY affected his choices and relationships in the story. How would the story have been different if Everett did not have this OE?

10. At the end of the book, Everett was at peace with his mother's decision to leave him. Do you think that she made the right choice? Why or why not?

Revelations: The School for Gifted Potentials, Volume 2
is now available!

With his ORIENTATION behind him, Everett is officially a Gifted Potential. Just as he is learning to juggle assignments, friends, and his myriad of emotions, an unexpected visitor to The School for Gifted Potentials is announced. The school transforms as the staff and students eagerly await their famous guest, but his visit stirs up new questions about Everett's past. What other secrets did his mother keep, and what will be revealed the longer Everett stays at the school that his mother had tried so desperately to keep him from?

Get your copy now!